Past's Prologue

What is known today will change the views of the past

written by
Nova Mitchell

PAST'S PROLOGUE

First Printing: 2014

ISBN 1494411369

www.novamitchell.com

DEDICATION

Dedicated to my Mother and Father, who have always
believed in me.

Special thanks to my husband, Sean, who gave me
encouragement throughout my random outburst and quirky acts.
To my writing buddies who indulge my crazy imagination. And
to Shiela Stone who - even after asking her to read the same
things many times over - always gave it another look.

PAST'S PROLOGUE

CHAPTER 1 : SCOTIA
= The Consequences of Curiosity =

It was early in the morning and I was spending my time in the stables of the Order. It's mostly quiet here and the stable men didn't bother me. I'm sure they wondered why I'd bother to spend time here, but I had my reasons and they never bothered to ask. The stable man choose instead to kept to their horses and cleaning out the muck. I am a Novilite of the Order and one day I will rise to the rank of a Ma'Tradom. We are able to control the natural elements - the Kenisis is what we called it - and while people knew that we contained ourselves from hurting innocents they were always wary of us.

I have been studying at the Order for eight years and my ability in the Kenisis was laughable at best. I would leave, but until I am able to past my trials and become a Proxi - the next level up - I was not allowed to leave. The Ma'Tradom's said I had trouble concentrating and was unable to focus well on the Kenisis that I wanted to wield. I know all the mechanics of how it is suppose to work but, after failing time and time again at anything above the basic level I didn't believe I could do anything more. I was resting against the horses' feed sacks in the back of the stable, trying to focus on seeing the strands of hay on the dirt floor blow over to the side with a gust of wind, but all I could see was the hay.

Suddenly I heard the chimes in the clock tower ring, they were sounding off the ninth hour. *How had it gotten to be so late already?* I started to focus again on the hay when I remembered that I had Geokenisis this morning. I had forgotten about the class and now I was going to be late. Hastily I dashed out the stables. If I hurried I could make it to my class before the Ma'Tradom realized I wasn't there.

I tried not to trip over my own feet as I ran as fast as I could up the grey marble staircases and down the brightly lit hallways of the Order. Lifting my long and heavy blue skirt up to my knees to allow my legs extra freedom I ran as fast as I could. I paid little attention to the other servants that were about, or the tapestries and artwork that adorned the walls of this old castle structure. The ending chimes of the hour beat at me from the large windows that I passed, mocking my attempts to get all the way to the fourth floor in time. Never before had the hallways seemed so vast as they did now.

I'm not going to make it! I prayed that no one from the Order would see me running. If a Ma'Tradom, or even a Proxi, caught me I'd be caned for sure. It was against the rules for a Novilite to run inside the Order unless their life were in immediate danger. This qualified as such a circumstance to me.

The chimes stopped right before I reached my destination and I skidded to a stop in front of the closed classroom door. Already late, there was nothing I could do about it now but hope that Ma'Tradom Aquali would not be too upset.

I hated this class. Geokenisis. Out of all the Kenisis offered this was my weakest. Wiping the sweat from my hands on my skirt I opened the door, but only enough for me to slip inside. All the classrooms had the students enter in at the back so anyone coming in wouldn't block the view of what was going on in the front. I never paid much attention to it before, but perhaps this could be my saving grace. The chimes had only recently ended, and if I could slip into one of the back seats I could pretend that I had always been here.

The students, other Novilites, stood behind polished wooden tables and the air smelled of wet soil and pine. I could feel the Kenisis energy flowing through the room. On the tables were pots of dirt and the Novilites had their fingers buried up to their knuckles in the soil of their pots. The bright sunlight from the windows bathed much of the room and my hope to go unnoticed vanished as soon as I stepped away from the doorway and into the light of the class.

"Late again, Scotia," Ma'Tradom Aquail said. Her cool gaze fixed on me from the front of the class. She was tall with sunken cheeks, and when she narrowed her eyes and glared at someone she looked almost like a snake. I imagined her hissing at me now.

I froze in place and everyone suddenly turned to look in my direction. I turned towards the Ma'Tradom, kneeled and bowed my head to the floor in the way we were taught. Never once did I raise my eyes to meet hers and never had I been so glad to look at the marble floor.

"Yes, Ma'Tradom," I answered, hoping that my voice came forth with more humility than fear of retribution. "I'm sorry, Ma'Tradom."

I felt the soft vibrations her steps made on the floor as the Ma'Tradom approached me. "Today marks the fourth time you have been late for my lessons. Are you unable to tell the time?"

"No, Ma'Tradom." My voice sounded soft, barely above a whisper. There wasn't another sound being made in the entire room, making my small voice loud in my ears. The others of the Novitiate knew better than to speak while a Ma'Tradom was disciplining, to do so would bring judgment on them as well. "I tell time rather well." I regretted my additional retort the moment it came out of my mouth, but I couldn't take it back.

"I see. So then you purposefully choose to ignore the hour and interrupt my lesson so that you can pull at your classmates attention," came the Ma'Tradom's accusation. "Or perhaps you're so advanced that you don't need my lessons."

I had kept my head down the entire time she spoke but now I ventured to look up and open my mouth to speak in my defense. I saw that she had already turned away from me and was approaching her spot at the front of the class. The others had turned away from me as well and were watching Aquail.

"Pay attention Novilites," the Ma'Tradom stated, "Scotia is going to show you all how to properly do today's assignment."

My heart sunk, I couldn't believe what was said. I was going to make a fool of myself in front of the entire class. I had failed to show anything more than the smallest spark of ability in the Geokenisis and she knew that. My heart was pounding, but I couldn't back down from a Ma'Tradom's request. Curling my fingers into a determined fist I stood and walked to the front of the class, keeping my eyes forward and attempting to focus on the task at hand.

Upon reaching the front I stood behind the Ma'Tradom's table. It was clean of anything but her pot. It was average in size, nothing much to mention, and filled completely with black dirt. A simple seed, I knew, was buried in there somewhere and it was my task to make it grow. At the very least produce a small sprout. We had been preparing for this part of the assignment for a couple days. One of the first things we were taught in Geokenisis was how to connect with the Earth. Become one with it, feel it coursing through your body and lend it your energy. It was something so basic that even those not strong in Geo could do. I had no problem when it came to connecting with the earth, it was in doing anything with it where my difficulty lied. I looked up and saw Ma'Tradom Aquila standing there with her arms crossed, waiting.

I pulled the pot towards me, placed my hands on the rim and looked down at the dirt, determined to show the Ma'Tradom and my classmates that I could do it. Easing my fingers into the dirt I took a deep breath. I felt the slight dampness of the soil against my skin and the life it contained. *Grow. Grow. Come on.* I focused as hard as I could on seeing this seed grow. Seeing the plant cracking open the shell and stretching up through the soil. It was going to work. I would make it work. Then, I felt the soil drying up around my fingers and the life in the soil was gone. This happened to me every time I tried to manipulate the earth. It was foolish to think that this time would be any different.

After my failed performance in Geo, Aquail sent me out of the classroom to scrub the long hallway floor outside the High Ma'Tradom's anti-chamber. I hated going there, but it was a lighter punishment than what I could have received. The floor here was always cold and the longer a persons skin was against it, the colder they got. It wasn't your typical cold like those of a winter in Arameyth, this floor was infused with the High Ma'Tradom's Kenisis energy and it left the body frigid even hours after the person was done with their task. There were no rugs here to absorb the chill and rumor had it that one of the Novitiate nearly froze to death during their sentenced punishment to clean the floor. After half an hour of work my fingers and hands were so cold that I could hardly feel the brush in my hands.

"By the Earth and Stars Scotia, you must stop being late to class all the time!"

"It's not my fault!" I protested over the scratching sounds our bristle brushes made as they scrubbed the stone floor of the High Ma'Tradom's anti-chamber.

Maerilea was the closest thing that I had to a friend at the Order, she was eighteen and older than me by two years. Very adept at the Kenisis she would soon face the trails to test out of the Novilite and become a Proxi. "You've got to get better at focusing on the task at hand. What if something had happened?"

I answered her question with a shrug, I didn't want to be reprimanded again. We worked in silence for a while and in the quiet I heard the sound of raised voices drifting out from underneath the High Ma'Tradom's room where a Council meeting was currently being held. How peculiar. I had scrubbed this floor before while there was a meeting in progress but they were never loud enough to be heard. Curiosity piqued and I wanted to see if I could make out what was being said. Putting down my brush I crawled closer to the door.

Maerilea saw what I was doing. "Have you completely lost your mind!" Maerilea whispered in rushed and frantic tones, but I was only giving her half an ear. "Eavesdropping on a meeting of the Council - or anything that goes on in that room for that matter. You'll be flayed alive!"

"Hush!" I whispered sharply back. I knew the consequences. "They have never been loud enough for their voices to travel out here before. They sound upset."

"And they'll be even more so if they open that door and find you sitting with your ear plastered to the other side!" Maerilea put down her brush and grabbed me by the arm to pull me back.

"Aren't you the least bit curious!" I protested.

"No, and that will keep me alive longer than you. Now, come on!" Maerilea's tug was harder that time and she jerked me away from the door. Maerilea stumbled back a few steps and knocked over my cleaning bucket. Dirty soapy water spilled out on the clean floor and the echo the bucket made bounced off the walls.

The talking in the High Ma'Tradom's room stopped and Maerilea and I were frozen in place out of fear. I saw the door knob turn.

"Quickly!" Maerilea urged as she rushed back to her bucket and brush. Fear of getting caught was a great motivator, and I scrambled to salvage what I could of my bucket and, after retrieving my brush, went to work on the spill. The High Ma'Tradom's door opened and out she came with an entourage of five other Ma'Tradoms. I worked hard to contain my fear and work on the floor that I felt growing colder by the second. The High Ma'Tradom was tall and slender, her silvery robes draped about her and pooled around her feet. She was known as the most powerful Kenisis wielder, able to control multiple elements at a time under the greatest pressure and not even bat an eye. She began walking towards us, and the water on the floor turned to ice. I was freezing, but I made no attempt to warm myself.

The tension in the hallway was so thick that I found it hard to breathe. My lungs were growing tight and the cold drilled its way to my core. Finally, the High Ma'Tradom spoke. "Do you think that I would not know that you were at my door? Listening." I couldn't feel my fingers on the brush, I couldn't feel anything, nor could I move. Off to the side I heard Maerilea begin to moan in pain.

"Take them both," the High Ma'Tradom said. The air was pulled from my lungs and I passed out.

I don't know how long I was out, or what time it was when I regained consciousness. I tried to open my eyes but they were covered. I tried to move only to find that my hands were tied behind my back and my feet bound at the ankles. The floor was solid underneath me and it didn't have the cold of the High Ma'Tradom's antechamber.

I grew up in the Order, washing the floors and doing chores around the structure long before I was old enough to train in the Kenisis. I knew the halls probably better than anyone and could tell the rooms apart simply by the feel in the air. But this room felt new, unlike any other in the Order I had been in before. I couldn't sense anything here and there was a low hum whistling around my head that made it harder to maintain what little focus I had.

What was going on here? Why was I bound and what had happened to Maerilea? I had only been trying to listen in on something that was none of my business, surely that cannot be grounds for something like this!

Cautiously I called out, "Maerilea? Maerilea, are you there?" The answer came in the form of a nearly inaudible muffle heard on the outside of the humming in my head. Could that be her? I hoped it was and took it as a positive sign: she was here and I was not alone.

"I can't hear you," I said. The muffle was the only other sound I heard aside from the humming and so I considered us to be alone but was to afraid to raise my voice higher. "What's going on? Where are we?"

There was nothing to feel but the floor and nothing to hear but the sounds around my head. I couldn't even feel the Kenisis or concentrate enough to try. Maybe this was the Dead-box. The thought of that turned my stomach into lead and a more fearful feeling settled over me. I pulled my knees into my chest and sought to get a hold of the rapid beating of my heart.

##

When the only company you have is yourself, and the only light you have is in your memories, time is irrelevant. One hour, eight hours, a day, a week, even the concept of night and day don't hold any purpose when there is no way of distinguishing one from the other. I thought my ears would bleed from the constant humming; and panicking had drained me of my strength. At some point I laid down on the hard floor - I didn't try to roll or scoot anywhere. Eventually I started getting hungry. I guess you could say that hunger allowed me to keep track of the time. I started to count how many times my stomach rumbled. This went on for so long that my body forgot to be hungry. The rumbling stopped and that indicator of time was lost.

I can't remember when it was that the humming stopped, all I know is that when it did the next thing I heard were the sounds of footsteps on the floor and frantic screaming from Maerilea. Someone was here.

"Maerilea!" I yelled, my voice coarse, cracked, and weak. I swallowed hard a few times to induce moisture and coughed. I hadn't realized how dry it had become. "Maerilea!" I got up quickly and fell back down, landing roughly on the floor. My arms and legs were stiff and sore from being unable to move them for so long. "Who's here?"

Hands grabbed my upper arm and pulled me roughly to my feet and held me there. If it wasn't for that I would have fallen back down to my knees. The grip was strong and secure. I felt like a sore rag doll, depleted of energy and with a will that was nearly broken, but I tried to focus on the situation.

There had to be at least three people here with us: the one holding me, another holding Maerilea and someone who had directed them to do so. I wished the humming was back, I didn't want to hear the distress that was in the voice of my friend. Neither of us would be here if I had only listened to her and stayed away from the door. It was all my fault. My throat choked up and my eyes began to tear under my blindfold as I started to cry. I had never experienced anything like this.

"Stop crying. There is no room for tears in the Order." The commanding voice of the one holding me was stern, and I did my best to comply.

They pulled on my arms and I tried to walk more than be dragged to wherever I was going. Luckily it wasn't more than a few steps. I was told to sit and after I had done so, my arms were let go. My head was yanked forward and the blindfold was removed.

I squeezed my eyes shut first before I tried to open them, internally needing to encourage myself to be able to open my eyes. I was afraid of what I would see or, even worse, what I wouldn't see. When I opened them I saw floors, walls, and a ceiling that were completely black with the only source of light coming from the open door on the other side of the room. I was reminded of what I felt when I first arrived here.

This room was empty. It could only have been the Dead-Box.

Our captors wore silver veils that covered their faces from the eyes down and their robes were grey and unmarked. They didn't want to be known. Maerilea was sitting next to me and she reached out and took my hand in hers, giving it a squeeze. Though I had gotten her into this mess she whispered words of encouragement to me, saying that things would be okay.

I did not believe her and I couldn't understand why they had treated us so when all we did was try to eavesdrop. I didn't see the purpose behind it and even now that we were free from our restraints they did not offer anything in the way of answers. No one spoke at all.

The light from the door was blocked as someone else made their way into the room. No robes hung off of her body nor did she wear a bell-sleeve top and full skirt of the other Ma'Tradoms. She wore fitted black pants and a blood red corset, high lace boots on her feet and, though they had heels, they made no noise as she walked across the tiled floors. My eyes grew wide, recognition of the woman sparked in the forgotten recesses of my mind. She crossed gloved arms across her stomach and light glinted off the braided dull metal band that circled her left arm under the shoulder which marked her as a Ma'Tradom. Silver bracelets were on either wrist.

I shook my head in disbelief at what was brought to life in front of me. I found my voice and spoke in disbelief. "What are you doing here?"

CHAPTER 2: SCOTIA
= To Ravensbro =

My mother, Ma'Tradom Airtia, gave no reply to my question. I couldn't believe she was here. I have not seen her since she took my brother and I from our home eight years ago and she dropped me off here at the Order. I was too young to begin any training then and spent my earlier years working about the place as a servant. The only communications I had from her were from a few short and vague letters.

"Mother? Mother, what's going on?" I asked again, but still she didn't reply.

My mother nodded to the veiled Ma'Tradoms and they lifted Maerilea and I off the ground and began dragging us from the room. Confused to what was going on I looked behind me to see if my mother was going to come with us, but she didn't. I wasn't sure how much I could walk, my legs felt weak and my head dizzy.

The hallways were strangely empty, even the servants were gone. We were taken down to the clinic on the main floor. There were no windows in the clinic. There were a few beds and tables with medical supplies. Light and heat came from the bulbs along the walls. There was no one else in the room but us. After we were inside they left and Maerilea and I alone. We looked at each other for a moment and then Maerilea went to the washroom. After a few moments I heard the water turn on. I left her alone and laid down on one of the beds and fell asleep in a matter of minutes.

For two days we were kept in the clinic. Now and then a veiled Ma'Tradom would come in to give us food and another one would check on our health. I found it ironic that they were concerned for our well being now after having us blindfolded and tied up. Any questions I asked the Ma'Tradoms went unanswered and my frustrations only grew. We passed the time by working on the Kenisis. Maerilea tried to help me learn to focus better but the only thing I could think about was my mother and wonder what was happening and why was she here.

At the start of the third day, two Ma'Tradoms came into the Clinic to escort us out. During the walk I had never seen the halls so empty and quiet that I was convinced that they only moved us when they were sure that any others would not see. Aside from the four of us there wasn't anyone to see or hear as we made the trek. Where had everyone gone? I had thought that we were finally being taking back to our rooms in the residency quarter of the Order and given over to training once again, but that wasn't the case. Instead, they took us to the front doors.

I had always seen someone at the doors before but now there was only my mother. In her arms were a pair of long white cloaks. I recognized them as part of the garments given to Novilites when they graduated to Proxi, the next level up. The cloaks symbolized their ability to leave the Order. Proxis were also given silver bands which were fused around their wrist. We were told that these acted as a conduct for our focus as we trained outside the Order.

As mother placed the cloaks on our shoulders Maerilea and I murmured our thanks. We did not receive the silver bands. I opened my mouth to question why, but a look from the other Ma'Tradom's that had accompanied us caused me to reconsider. Once we were fitted in our cloaks the veiled Ma'Tradoms opened the front doors. This was the first time I had seen outside world since I ran to class from the stables. I still wasn't sure exactly how many days had passed since then, but right now it was dusk and the sky never looked so beautiful. Outside waiting for us was a black carriage. I had seen these come to the Order before. They were very well-made with springs on the wheel axels to soften the bumps of the road. The insides were said to be lavish with velvet curtains and the softest cushions ever felt. Two primped white horses were at the front of the carriage and a well tailored coachman in reds and gold sat in the seat. A footman, similarly dressed, stood at the carriage door. These carriages were the transportation of choice for the Governor of Oasedle, the main city in Arameyth. The Order resided a few miles south of the city, near a mountain range that marked the end of the South Kingdom.

The footman opened the carriage doors. "Get in. Both of you," directed my mother and Maerilea and I complied, leaving out the gates of the Order and going into the carriage. We sat together on the plush bench. The interior of the carriage was just as grand as I imagined. Ma'Tradom Airtia entered too and sat across from us and the carriage door closed. I didn't know if she was the reason why my friend and I were held in that cursed room for so long or if she was to thank for our release; part of me said she was both our punisher and savior.

I heard the reigns clack and the carriage started moving. We were leaving. Had everything back at the Order been a test? The torturous isolation and fear, were they nothing but a trial to see if we were ready? It couldn't have been. They knew how badly I had preformed in Geo and I was only minimally better in the others. I was confused as to why were were being taken away and what was to become of us now.

The ride was long. At first I had thought that it would only be an hour, maybe even two, before we stopped for a respite but we kept going. The carriage had four windows, two on either side. Looking out of them to see the scenery would have been a welcomed relief if they had not been drawn shut by heavy curtains. Ambient sounds filtered through the windows of the carriage as we passed through Arameyth. Sometimes I'd hear people greet the coachmen as we went by and he would reply with civility as we passed, but eventually they faded.

Everything was quiet inside of the carriage. Maerilea and I maintained close contact, sticking together and averting our eyes from my mother who sat watchfully across from us. It was deeply unnerving to me. I looked at the darkened pattern of the carriage walls and seats for so long and so hard that there patterns were undoubtedly a permanent fixture in my mind. I used the time on the road to practice focusing, but there were so many distractions that I had trouble focusing on one thing.

The silence and monotony of travel was hypnotizing and I wavered in and out of consciousness during the trip, my body wanting to give in to the recent stresses and retreat into itself. My confidence and faith in myself to be able to do anything to help this situation faded with every turn of the carriage wheel.

"There is something you girls need to know," Ma'Tradom Airtia said into the silence.

The words came quite suddenly that Maerilea and I both were startled. Mother saw the looks on our faces but carried on in what she was going to say. "Talks of war are circulating throughout the Four Kingdoms."

War wasn't unheard of in the Four Kingdoms and the next election was three years away. The Kings Chair was something that every Governor wanted. It established them as King and their Kingdom as the leader of the Realms. Homage was paid to that King and they made the laws and controlled the Kings Guard, an elite fighting force second only to the Masters. Every ten years the ruling Governors of four Kingdoms petitioned for the Kings Chair and those petitions often lead to civil wars. Talk of war wasn't good news, yet it wasn't dramatic news either.

"The two of you are being given to Governor Rycliff of Certima in the Eastern Kingdom of Tassone to assure he becomes King in the coming election."

I was surprised at how nonchalant my mother sounded. "What do you mean?" asked Maerilea, her voice filling with fear and panic. She clenched her skirt with her right hand and leaned forward in her chair. "You mean sold? Like, like slaves!"

This could not be true, the Order wouldn't sell their own - especially not for a persons political gain. The Ma'Tradoms were not suppose to use their abilities for selfish reasons. I inched closer to my friend and took her arm, huddling against it as much for her sake as it was for mine.

"As students of the Order you should be aware that there are certain things that must be done." My mother replied.

The apparent lack of care in her voice was astounding. I couldn't believe what was being said. I mouthed the word 'sold' but nothing was verbally spoken. Slavery. It wasn't uncommon in the Four Kingdoms; we learned about it in our studies. Oasedle, the main city in the Southern Kingdom - and location of the Governors palace - was the main hub for slave trade in the Realms. Depending on who owned you being a slave varied in treatment and what you were able to do. But no matter how you were treated, if you were a slave you were property and marked in some way that everyone knew that you were not your own person.

How could a Ma'Tradom be a slave? Nowhere in the books I've read or lessons we've been taught was there any mentioning of items or people being able to force these powerful women to do anything. If we were being given to Governor Rycliff of Certima then he had to have figured out a way, and that would make him a very dangerous man.

I was thrown to the floor when Maerilea suddenly jumped from her seat and sprang at the carriage door. She pulled at the handle trying to open it and make her escape.

"Maerilea!" I shouted, believing that the door would fly open and my friend would be lost to me to the world outside.

"Don't be foolish," said Ma'tradom Airtia. Maerilea grunted and was thrown back from the door and landed against the floor. My mother must have had the carriage door sealed and likewise pushed my friend back by using an element of the Kenisis. She hadn't moved from her seat.

"You can't do this to us!" came Maerilea's protest. "We can't be battered and sold, we're of the Order!" The words ended in tears as my friend started to cry.

Are we still part of the Order, I wondered. *The way we were treated, how we were taken from it. We didn't even get our bracelets.*

Mothers eyes bore holes into both of us. "Do not question things for which you have no understanding."

I started to shiver. Small shakes traveled down my body as I felt the weight of my mothers eyes watching me. I couldn't look at her but I wanted to say something. I wanted to yell and question why she'd sell her own daughter into slavery. This couldn't be how the Order did business, if it was then how many other girls had been sold? My protest stayed internal and for a while more the only sounds were that of the carriage wheels turning upon the road and Maerilea's sobs.

It would take nearly two weeks to travel to Certima at the pace we were going. We slept in the carriage as well as ate. The only time we stopped was to buy more food and to relieve ourselves.   Once, when we had stopped to stretch, Maerilea tried to run away but she was unable to go more than a few feet past the carriage. It had to be another one of mothers tricks, though I couldn't fathom the Kenisis she used. She hadn't even been watching when Maerilea tried to escape.

During the trip we were encouraged to practice our Kenisis, but neither Maerilea or I made much progress. Mother had loosed the hold upon the windows and we were able to look out at the land as we passed. Though I was grateful to have something else to look at besides the walls and floor of the carriage it came with many distractions, and what my mother had said hung over me.

As night began to fall on the third day, we pulled into Ravensbro. The city rested near the border between Oasedle and the Eastern Kingdom of Tassone. Ravensbro had a small sea port from which they accepted trades from the Lands Beyond the Sea and because of this, even in the darkening hour, sounds of a bustling community could be heard outside the carriage door. A few more miles to the east and we would take the path that crossed over the chasm and enter Tassone.

Maerilea was sleeping against the wall. I pulled back one of the window curtains to take a peek. Street lamps were in the process of being lit, sellers were hawking the last of their wares, and people were either heading home or to a tavern to spend more of the evening. The air was a mixture of ocean and city life, something that I had never experienced before. A waif of smoke from a passing lit lamp made me cough enough that I closed the curtain and sat back down inside. I wished it were day, at least then I would have been able to see the city more clearly.

The carriage slowed to a stop and the coachman exchanged words with someone outside. I started to listen but had my attention disturbed when my mother started talking.

"You understand why this is happening don't you, Scotia?" She said.

I sunk back in my seat like a sulky child and crossed my arms. "No. No I don't understand why you took us from the Order and are making us slaves for some silly war that we're not even a part of."

"Have they taught you nothing?" mother asked. "Or have your ears and eyes been so against what is there for you to know."

The carriage started again.

"I know plenty ---."

"Then stop sitting there like an irreverent child." The words had sounded hard and by the look in her eyes I could tell that she was starting to loose patience with me. It was the same look that Aquali and the other Ma'Tradoms gave me when they thought I was being testy or insubordinate. Without thought I straightened my back and sat proper, though I kept my arms crossed and averted my eyes to look to my mothers left. There was nothing that I wanted to say, and her words seemed ended for the moment as well. We sat in silence until the carriage stopped again.

Maerilea woke up, though whether from the pitched stopped of our transportation or the lively music that that came through the windows was unsure. Perhaps we had arrived at an Inn. After sleeping uncomfortably in the carriage the thought of actually being in a bed was delightful. The carriage rocked and I heard the coachman speaking to someone outside. Maerilea and I exchanged glances and then looked at the door expecting it to open. After being stuck inside for hours both of us were eagerly wanting to give a proper stretch to our legs.

"Listen to me carefully, girls," there was a cautionary tone in my mothers voice and we turned to listen. "Once you leave this carriage you are to keep your mouths sealed. Talk to no one and look at no one directly. Do not leave my side. Is this understood?"

"Yes, Ma'Tradom." Maerilea and I said together. Mother spoke as if we were not safe, though surely we were. Who would be foolish enough to attack someone from the Order? Ravensbro may house an eclectic group of people, but it was never said to be a threat to the Order. It would not make sense to stop here if it was.

My mother put herself between us and the opening door and stepped out first, Maerilea took my hand and led me out. The sign above the door marked the establishment as 'The Wayward Man', a three story building with a stone and wood facade and five steps that went up to the front door. For a split moment I thought about running; dragging Maerilea along. I wondered if we would be able to get past the carriage, considering what happened when Maerilea had tried to run. Mother was already stepping inside the inn and the footman stood behind me to block any escape.

Before we entered, our Proxi cloaks were taken from us by the coachman and stored away in trunks. Maerilea and I looked like well-kept young ladies. Without our cloaks there was nothing to mark who we really were. As for my mother, the only defining Ma'Tradom item she had were the silver bands on her wrist and the braided band under her shoulder. Still, we did not look like a rag-tag group as we entered the inn. We were hiding ourselves to blend in - that is how it appeared. The question still remained as to why. Who would threaten the Order?

I noticed that a few eyes looked in our direction more than once, but that could have simply been because we brought cold air with us when the door opened. The revelry of the inn was much louder on the inside. A brightly dressed fiddler plucked merrily upon his strings to a tune that had the taverns patrons singing along as they clapped their hands and stomped their feet. Some men even circled the floor with a woman in their arms. Loud chatter and merriment was everywhere. The whole place felt washed in contagious euphoric energy that brought a smile to my face. I had never seen anything like this before, such celebration and lax of inhibition never happened in the Order. As we made our way to an empty table and sat down I temporarily forget about my current situation.

##

During dinner I tried to do what my mother had told us to do in the carriage: keep our mouths shut and don't look at anyone directly. But it wasn't easy. My senses were going crazy and sometimes a person would push against me as they went past the table. If anyone lingered too long by us the coachman gave them a look that changed their mind. I thought I heard whispers of people questioning who we were, but I couldn't be sure. I didn't see any Ma'Tradoms in the room, but I did notice a pair of skinny men by the front door who kept looking in our direction. Mother noticed me looking and followed my eyes. I looked away and buried my attention into my nearly finished bowl of cabbage and potato soup. She didn't say anything to me about my looking, only leaned towards the footman and whispered in his ear. When I looked back up later the two men were gone. It's probably for the best, I thought.

Out of all of us at the table, Maerilea was the most relaxed. It surprised me. She looked happy and I even caught her foot tapping a time or two to the songs played on the stage. I wanted to join in on the fun and relax, but I also wondered where those men had gone off to.

The good spirit that had resided downstairs vanished after dinner when Maerilea and I were taken to a room on the third floor where we were to stay for the night. It was not much larger than my room at the Order, it had a small bed with a thin mattress, an old chair and side table. With the trunks that our coachmen placed into the room our space was a bit tight, but it was luxury after the small space of the carriage. There was a window that faced the street and I looked out of it and saw only a few straggling villagers meandering around between the buildings. The coachman and footman were set as guards outside our door and that made me feel uneasy.

"You two should get some rest while you can," Ma'Tradom Airtia said as she secured the door and pulled up a chair to sit besides it.

Maerilea fell asleep easily, stating that the events of the day had taken their toll. I tried, but sleep alluded me for many hours. I couldn't get comfortable on the bed, even if it was better than sleeping on the carriage seat. I watched my mother for a bit. There were so many things I wanted to ask her, but I couldn't find the courage to do so.

Eventually I feel asleep and shortly after a loud crash outside our door, followed by yelling, woke both myself and Maerilea. Beyond the door came the sound of steel upon steel.

"Dress yourselves, quickly!" Mother commanded. She was standing and waiting at the door, her hands up and ready to attack whatever may be on the other side. We scrambled to do as we were told, stuffing our feet into shoes and tugging tunics and cloaks over our heads. The noise in the hallway was getting louder and more violent, I could feel my heart bursting out of my chest. There were screams outside the door and we were trapped inside. Death was outside that door.

"When I say 'run', I want you girls to run out of here as fast as you can," Airtia said. "Get a horse and ride hard for the Governor's Palace in Certima. Don't let anything stop you from going there."

"What about you!" Maerilea shrieked as our door buckled under some unknown force. "We can help!"

"You will do as I say!" Ma'Tradom Airtia shouted back.

Our door broke apart, the debris scattered about the room. In the doorway were four grossly oversized men with black hoods pulled down over their faces. Their bodies soaked in the light from the room and around their waist I saw a Masters symbol - a golden lightening bolt surrounded by a metal ring. This didn't make sense. The Masters wouldn't attack innocent people, especially not Ma'Tradoms.

The men charged in. "RUN!" shouted mother and with a quick motion of her hands the attackers were slammed against the wall. This was our way out, the only moment we would have. Mother shouted at us, "Run! Go now! Hurry!" She wouldn't be able to hold them for long. No matter how strong you were, sooner or later something broke your concentration and focus. The less you were able to concentrate the weaker your Kenisis became until you couldn't hold it at all.

Maerilea grabbed my hand and we ran pass the men and out the door to find the hallway was awash with destruction. Blood stained the floor and ceiling. The other doors in the hallway were bashed in and mangled bodies could be seen thrown about. These people had been butchered. My knees shook and Maerilea looked ready to pass out but the sound of things breaking and the scream that came from our room spurred us to keep going. My mother was back there, but there was nothing that I could do to help her if I went back.

The steps were slippery and we fell a time or two in our rush to get down. We stopped at the bottom of the steps. The bar was fully ablaze and so was the front door, but we couldn't stay here. Heavy footsteps came from above.

"They're coming!" I yelled.

"What are we suppose to do, Scotia? We're trapped and those things are going to kill us for sure, just like they did the Ma'Tradom!"

She can't be dead. "We'll have to run through the fire." I found my courage from somewhere, maybe it was my resolve to believe that my mother was not dead.

Maerilea was panicking. "We'll get burned!"

"But we'll be alive! Now, go!" The heavy footsteps were getting closer. Maerilea and I covered as much of our faces as we could with our cloaks and bolted from the steps, through the inferno that had been the front door and out into the street.

Chaos was everywhere, clearly our tavern was not the only place that had been attacked. Screams echoed from the buildings and the streets were in such a frenzy that the action made me dizzy. Riding out of the city was not an option as we found the stable was burnt to the ground and the horses gone. We held tightly to each others hands and ran. We ran as far away from 'The Wayward Man' and Ravensbro as fast as we could.

CHAPTER 3: TYLAN
= Only The Strong Survive =

Crack!

The fist slammed into the center of my face and broke my nose. The roar of the crowd watching from atop of the high stonewalls intensified and my vision blurred. I shuffled back a few steps and fought hard to stay on my feet. *I got to stay on my feet,* I thought while shaking my head to work away the double vision. *Got to stay standing.*

It was the day of Tourney, one of the most important days for the boys training at the School of the Iron Fist, the Masters School in the Northern Kingdom of Barq. Myself and the other 39 boys of the Third Tier, Fledglings we were called, had been assembled in the training arena just after first light. Dressed in our loose fitting trousers and boots we were equipped with only our regulation dirk for a weapon. Once the tourney started we were to fight each other until only ten of us remained standing.

Fighting wasn't uncommon here. From the day you arrived at the school, and every day thereafter, you either fought back against those that attacked or you wished for death while having your bones broken as you cowered on the ground. The Masters school turned you into a fighter and a killer, even if they had to literally beat it into you.

The rules were of the Tourney were simple: fight until only ten of you are left standing. Once your back hit the ground you were considered out. Those who fell in the fight would endure the harsh penalty of the Masters whip. Worst of all, the branding you had received to signify that you survived the brutality of the first years at the school would be covered up. You would go back to being an Unmarked, starting again at the bottom.

At the School of the Iron Fist boys as young as eight years old were beaten nearly every day for a year by the Masters and the older boys as part of training. Learn to fight and survive by being in a constant state of ready seemed to be the motto here; if there was something else I was to learn then it alluded me. If at the end of those first years you were more dead than alive you were taken away. To where? No one knew for sure. Rumors said they were killed. Those who survived were given a dirk and initiated into the

School by having two lines burned under the shoulder of their right arm.

You were then Third Tier, a Fledgling, which was hardly any better than being an Unmarked. Aside from being starved, deprived of sleep, and engaging in dangerous weapon fights, a Third Tier had educational studies to pass. Ignorance and weakness were not tolerated in a Masters school.

The boys who survived the Tourney were branded again, this time with the schools symbol - an iron fist- underneath those two lines and the daily beatings would stop. Your training would become more focused and food and sleep would become more of a reality than a frivolous dream. Some boys were even lucky enough to be chosen to go with a Master on excursions beyond the School's high stone walls. Being in the Second Tier, a Tyro, was a coveted title that you were willing to kill for to achieve. Death would be better than repeating the years of hell.

I prepared my attack and when I heard the sound of a foot scrapping along the dirt behind me. I ducked down quickly. Using my hands to cover my face I tucked in to protect my body. We learned to be prepared for attacks from all sides as it wasn't uncommon for two, or even three boys, to gang up on one as a way to eliminate competition.

I spun around with a strike aimed at the boy nearest to me and caught him in the kidney, but I didn't stop there. Quick pivot and dirt was kicked to the face of the boy who had tried to come at me from behind and in his momentary state of blindness I cracked his jaw. I had a chance to back away from the closeness of my two opponents but I would risk engaging myself in one of the other bouts going on around me. I didn't need any more.

I felt my strength waning but I knew that just as I was tiring the other boys were as well. I barely blocked a kick intended for my side and was left wide open for the stomp to the back of my knee. I locked my jaw to fight against the pain and by sheer force of will I was able to hold my knee inches from the ground as I went down. I didn't think I'd have the energy to get up if I hit the dirt.

There was barely enough time for me to think as that attacker came at me again, but I was able to catch his foot and use his coming momentum to pull myself up and crack him in the ribs. He hit the ground.

Out.

I readied myself for another attack when I heard the shrill whistle sound off from atop the wall. The Tourney was over. The din of the crowd hushed and I looked around at the other boys who were still standing in the arena. Two boys - the one that I had knocked over and another one not to far off - were the only ones left not standing as they were the recently fallen, the others had been dragged off earlier. Two boys. I was that close to not being one of the ten. Though the fighting was over I didn't let down my guard, unsure of what was going to happen next I thought it better to be safe than risk slipping up.

The large metal and wood double doors that made up the entrance gate of the arena opened with the help of two large men pulling on either side. In walked the High-Lord Master. It was at that time that I relaxed my fist and shoulders and stood up as straight as I could while ignoring the trickle of blood from my broken nose and the pain that was scattered over the rest of my body. When you stood in front of a Master - especially the High-Lord Master - you didn't show signs of weakness.

He was a tall man. The High-Lord Master was broad of shoulder and had thick, heavy hands that could crush a man's throat without much effort. Imposing, that's what he was and his skin was richly tanned from the many years spent in the sun and scared from the battlefield. Strapped to his back were his twin hook blades and on his breastplate was the symbol of the Iron Fist. His eyes were always narrowed with a permanent look of anger. In all my years at the school I have never seen him smile or do as much as a gruff laugh. He held the highest position anyone could in the Masters Schools for not only did he have say over what went on at the Iron Fist, but he had governing authority over the other Masters Schools in the Realms.

We all held our ground as he looked at us in turn. No one dared to move until he ordered us to come together with a single wave of his hand. "Forty of you entered into the Tourney arena this morning and now only ten of you remain." His voice was deep and it bore down on the silence and made itself heard. "I suppose you think you're tough! What makes you better than those that failed?"

The silence that followed didn't last but for more than a few moments before Odestan - eighteen and a year older than me (he had fallen in the Tourney last time) spoke up. Unlike many of the other members of the Iron First, Odestan had long hair which he kept pulled back and in a braid. "We do not fail, High Lord Master!" It may have been obvious, what Odestan said, but he said it with conviction.

PAST'S PROLOGUE

"You do not fail!" the High-Lord Master repeated.

As if on cue the sound of cracking whips filtered through the air to be followed by muffled screams, punishment for those who failed had begun. The rest of the arena was empty as well. I didn't even realize when the spectators had left. The corner of my eye flinched and a ghost pain from past whippings stung my back. I had been whipped before for failing at a task.

"You...do not FAIL! You do not have pity for your fellow brothers who did not make it. There is no room for the weak." The blood from my nose was gathering between my lips but I dared not even lick it away. The others standing with me were in the same shape - if not worse - than I and none of us were trying to straighten our appearance. We all were still as we watched the High-Lord Master walk up and down the list with his hands behind his back. "They should be kissing your feet, thankful that you didn't kill them!"

The sound of something weighted being wheeled in our direction took my attention and I strained my peripheral vision to try and get a glimpse of it without turning my head. Soon a large cast iron pot with branding irons sticking out of the top, came into view. It was being rolled in on a wooden dolly by one of the Masters. I had seen this pot before when I had received my Fledgling markings - but I looked in wonderment at who was walking behind the Master.

It was a female. Since the day that my mother took my sister and I from our home and dropped me off here at the gates of the Iron Fist I had never seen another female. Everyone living and working in the School was male so to see a female after all this time came as quite a surprise. I had almost forgotten what they looked like. If I wasn't mistaken from my studies she was a Ma'Tradom of the Order - a group of select females who possessed the ability to control the Kenisis.

She was small and in her silver colored robes she looked delicate. I couldn't see her face because she wore a veil, but her dusk colored hair was pulled back tightly in a bun. How strange it was to see her here, walking confidently in the bloodstained arena as though it were a regal hall.

The High-Lord Master began to speak again, moving back from us by a few steps and letting the Master with the pot and the Ma'Tradom take places to his left. "Today, you no longer belong to the Third Tier, a Fledgling. You are Tyros, men of the Second Tier!"

29

In near unison we in the line hit a fist over our heart twice and gave off a loud "Ho!" That was a sign of agreement. Tyro. How good it felt to finally make the rank.

"Henceforth you shall be marked and all that see you will fear the strength and destructive might that you possess!" The High-Lord Master continued, "They will marvel at how delicate you can be when you possess such power! For you are the ones that will control this world and form it!"

His words were inspirational and I felt my chest swelling with pride. I wanted to cheer. I wanted to roar loud enough that those boys being beaten in the rooms underneath the arena would hear me. I didn't care about my broken nose anymore or the pain over the rest of my body. None of it mattered right now.

"Come now and be marked." The High-Lord Master ushered forth the first boy in the line. I knew him. His name was Chulin, and he was heavy even with the lack of food we were given. He walked up to the pot and extended his right arm. The Master pulled the branding rod out and we all could see, even in the dimming light, that the black metal burned bright orange. The Ma'Tradom stepped beside Chulin and gripped his elbow in her hand. I didn't know what she was doing but I noticed how Chulin suddenly stood taller and was more composed than I had ever seen him. When the branding iron hissed against his skin Chulin didn't even flinch. When it was done he stood behind the High-Lord Master and I studied him. I studied him and the other four boys who were branded before me, each of them looking slightly different than they had before the Ma'Tradom had held their arm and the brand was placed.

Then it was my turn and I stood before the Master with the iron and the Ma'Tradom took my arm just as she did all the others. I felt a power rush through my body. It took away every pain that I had and made me a new creature full of strength such as I had never known. I was rested. I was alert. I felt like I could conquer the world. When the branding iron was placed against my arm I was detached from the pain and my heart felt hardened. The iron was removed but the Ma'Tradom continued to hold on to my arm. She was looking at me and in her eyes I saw fear. It was not there when she arrived, neither was it there when I saw her work on the other boys. But it was there with me. The Ma'Tradom slowly released my arm. I still felt that power burning inside of my chest as I took my rightful place in line behind the High-Lord Master.

PAST'S PROLOGUE

When this day started I was merely Tylan, another boy in the Masters School of the Iron Fist. Now I was Tyro Tylan, and I was on my way to becoming a Master.

##

It was now two weeks after the Tourney and life at the school couldn't have been more different for me. I wasn't starving all the time and meat started to form on my otherwise lankly body. I shared a barracks room with the others that had passed with me and we were given padded cots to sleep on and a blanket, this was a big difference over a cold, hard floor where you slept wherever you could find space. The ten of us were brothers for life now, Fledglings who went into battle together and came out as Tyros. We were to fight each other to beat out the weaknesses and push each other forward when we fell behind in our courses. If one of us got in trouble we all were punished. We needed to learn to be one cohesive unit but, in that unit, one of us would show ourselves to be the leader, the Sachem of our group. We could remain Tyros for up to five years. When the High-Lord Master thought that we were ready our Tyro would be tested again so that we could advance to the final rank and become Masters. At that point the Council of Masters - a collection of Lord Masters from each of the four kingdoms Masters Schools - would appoint the Sachem of our group. The Sachem was the leader of the group and was responsible for the men under his command.

As I walked with Odestan through the halls to our next class, Stratagem, I rubbed at the branding on my arm to remove the bits of scabbing that still remained. We all had the same classes but not at the same time, it was the Masters way of seeing how we worked with the different people of our Tyro and the other groups that had not yet graduated to Master. It was their way of seeing our personalities come forth. Odestan didn't seem like a talker - and I guess compared to others he wasn't - but whenever it was just the two of us he could talk on and on. I had more classes with him than any of the others.

"Did you hear? There's talks of wars in the West," he said, a smirk on his face.

"Yeah, so," I said as I shrugged my shoulders. A new King of the Realms would be picked in a few more years. A war to decide the outcome was almost natural.

"So?" Odestan said as he backhanded me in the chest, "so we might get to go on a scouting excursion!"

Odestan's statement would have made more sense to me if we had our ranking for more than two weeks, but we were still fresh. "I want a chance to step outside these walls as much as the next person, Odestan, but I think --" I started to say, and then was interrupted.

"Then stop thinking!" He stopped right there in the hall and put a hand on either of my shoulders. Our classroom door was in sight. "Gods man, you've said that you want to get out of these walls so act like it! You can't form the world from behind a wall, you have to get out there. There's nothing for us here. Nothing."

He pushed me back but I remained on my feet. What had gotten into him so suddenly, I wondered. Odestan walked backwards towards the classroom door and before he turned around he pointed his finger at me and said: "I'm going to get out there, and you're coming with me, so man up."

We were just in time for class.

"Sanjaen, gather up your men, it's time we made a move," the High-Lord Master gave the order to his First-Master. A thick skinned and burley man who kept his head shaved to hide the gray, Sanjaen was next in line to take over the school and was often the High-Lord Master's first choice when it came to passing assignments. He was quick, accurate, and it was said that no one in any of the Masters Schools was as good with a bow.

The council of Masters was gathered in the Great Hall of the school. One of the larger rooms at the Iron Fist the walls were made of grey brick and lined with banners that held the symbols of the four schools along with pictures and maps of each kingdom. The Masters were standing around a thick wooden table. A map stretched over the top and rolled scrolls and miniature battle figures rested along the side. What Odestan had heard was not a rumor, it was fact. The Governor of the Southern Kingdom had conspired with the Governor of the West to divide the Eastern Kingdom and dispose of it's Governor, Rycliff, before making a full on attack to the Northern Kingdom. It is most powerful one of the four and current holder of the King's Chair. There were four Masters Schools, one in each Kingdom, though the men in it we're not the soldiers or personal army of that Kingdoms ruling authority.

Masters were outside the law and yet were the very reason laws were around. At this meeting the Lord Masters of the schools in the South and West were missing,

The fact that war talks had broken out in the lands was not what caused this particular Council session, but it was the fact that the Lord Masters of the South and West were said to be leading the armies. There had to be something more to the war than the King's Crown. The Masters lived by a set of pre-established codes that had been in place since the first High-Lord Master was established hundreds of years ago - and though it may seem that the Masters worked to the benefit of one group or another, in the end it was for the betterment of all.

"I want to know what the blazes is going on out there." The High-Lord Master curled his fingers into fist and leaned down on the corners of the map. "Aligning with any Governor goes against our code."

Muttered words of agreement filtered around the room. First-Master Drakar, from the Eastern School, tossed in his opinion and spoke above the din of the others. "Perhaps they are uniting over greed..." When he trailed off his grey eyes flickered to Sanjean, who stood nearly directly across from him.

Before he continued First-Master Drakar placed a finger on the map and drew an invisible line from the Master School of the West to the one in the East. "The conditions in the West are not quite as easy as what you have here."

The lands of the West were dessert, yet there was a thriving kingdom in spite of the harsh sun and the dangerous creatures that roamed. Most of their economy came from trading with the other Kingdoms, especially Oasedle. It was no secret that the Lord Master of the Western School was envious of the East but he also, in his vanity, wanted to take control of all the schools. He wanted to be the High-Lord Master.

Lord Master Lantain, from the Masters School in East, slammed his fist down on the table and leaned towards his First-Master. "If the West wants to challenge me over rule of position he can face me like the Master he's suppose to be instead of hiding behind the force of thousands of men!" A war amongst the schools, thought Lantain, there hadn't been one in hundreds of years.

"What are you all standing around here for!" The High Lord Master barked, "Go get me some answers!"

"Yes, High-Lord Master." They all replied in unison and began leaving the Hall.

"Not you, Sanjean." The High-Lord Master said as he studied the map on the table. "Stay a moment."

"Yes, Sir," the First-Master said, hanging back as he let the others leave and waiting patiently for what the High-Lord was going to say.

Once he was sure that the others had gone, the High Lord Master spoke. "The Lotarians are back. I promised Tylan's mother when she left him here that I would keep him safe. But with what is coming, he cannot stay here."

First-Master Sanjean nodded his reply. "What do you propose?"

"Take him, and that group of Tyros, with you over the mountains and to the Western Kingdom," said the High-Lord.

Sanjean was surprised. "That group is not ready to leave the school. They will die out there."

The High-Lord Master looked up from the map and set his eyes on Sanjean. "We don't have the luxury, like the other Kingdoms, to easily get aid when trouble comes. If the Lotarians find out that the boy is here they will destroy this kingdom to find him. Let him go and face whatever fate has in store for him. As long as it's not here in my school."

"Yes, High-Lord Master." With that said Sanjean left the Great Hall.

##

It was break time and the rest of the Tyro and I were in the training yard practicing what we had learned in classes earlier that day. The Masters schools didn't believe in using models for us to practice with, either you paid attention on how to block the attack or you were injured. The only time an attack was held was when the Master showed a killing blow as there was no benefit to purposely kill the ones you trained. The Schools physicians were always on call.

My ribs were currently wrapped tightly from practice with Odestan earlier. I had over extended my reach and he had taken the advantage. It was a lucky shot and I made him pay for it with cracking his shoulder. Both of us would have been unable to fight for a while if it had not been for the physician that patched us up enough so we could continue and remember to be more careful.

Although, while I still showed signs of my injury Odestan looked to be in no pain at all.

First-Master Sanjaen came into the training yard followed by the men of his Cabal. Only men in the First-Masters group were given this ranking. They were considered to be the schools 'special forces'; the best of the best. From a starting force of ten - as in any Tyro - this Cabal was down to six.

The training stopped as we saw them approaching and we held ourselves in a position of readiness with our shoulders back and heads high, our eyes looking at theirs. After years of being punished for giving eye contact, to have to do so now did not come easily, but we were no longer Fledglings and were required to look the Masters in the eyes.

Steadily we moved in closer together as the Cabal formed a ring around us. I saw Chulin's fingers twitching on the spear he held in his hand; perhaps his thought was the same as mine. They were going to attack us, what other reason were they here?

I kept as many of the Masters in my vision as I could but my main focus was on First-Master Sanjaen. No one said anything and no one moved; and the quiet started to set me on edge. Soon Sanjaen's voice cut through the silence. "Which one of you is the leader?"

Leader? There was no leader in this Tyro. It hadn't been long enough for anyone to push up towards that position. We in the group looked at one another with the same question in everyone's eyes, wondering who was going to answer and what was going to happen to that person.

"Stop looking at each other and answer me!" The First-Master bellowed and all of our attention snapped back to him. "Give me an answer Tyros, or else have the answer beat out of you. Which one of you is the leader!"

The Cabal shifted their weight in anticipation of a fight, they looked anxious for it even.

"I am, First-Master Sanjaen," came the strong and clear voice of Kaleo. He was one of the older boys in the group, nineteen, and the only one of us who was able to free themselves of this temporary muteness. There was whisper of accent in his deep voice. "My name is Kaleo."

A single brow of Sanjaen's rose when Kaleo spoke up and he moved a step towards him while motioning that Kaleo do the same. "Kaleo, ready your Tyro. You all will travel with my Cabal and I to the Masters School in the West. Get your things packed.

We leave at first light." There was not going to be any more information than that for Sanjean turned and walked away, his men following.

We didn't move until they were nearly out of the yard then everyone took a breath. I noticed the others who had been practicing in the yard were looking at us but we didn't pay them much attention, instead the nine of us were looking at Kaleo and he was looking at us. The Sachem was picked by the Council, it wasn't self-appointed, so did his appointment count? At the moment I wasn't going to question the validity because I didn't want to be in his position.

"You all heard him.," Kaleo said while looking at all of us. "Let's get ready."

After the meeting in the yard we went to our barracks. Kaleo took up the lead and since he didn't talk none of us did either, that is until the door closed and it was only the ten of us in the room.

"Mind telling us what that was all about, Kaleo?" Samir said, the subtle anger in his voice was obvious to anyone. He was a year younger than Kaleo but slightly taller and broad whereas the other boy was thinner. A spark of tension was rising in the room that wasn't easily ignored. I stopped in packing my things for the trip. It would only take a second anyway, the only possessions I had were a few pieces of clothing, leather bracers for my arms and shin guards, my dirk, and the shoes on my feet.

Kaleo faced Samir, his face was straight and his eyes were challenging. From the time we became Fledglings we each developed our own looks of defiance and of challenge, it was something that happened naturally after being beaten and abused all the time. It was a look that told your opponent that you weren't afraid of them and were prepared for whatever was about to come. For some of us this look came and went, but for Samir it always seemed there on his face. "You have a problem with something, Samir?" Kaleo said.

"What gives you the right to be the leader?" Samir asked, bearing down on the shorter man.

"Unlike the rest of you sods I'm not afraid to speak up to a Master," Kaleo said, stepping up to Samir and lessening the distance. He cracked his neck while keeping the dead set lock of his eyes on Samir, his tone patronizing. "Found your voice now that he is gone?"

"Come on you guys," Odestan piped in, "if First-Master Sanjaen knows of this he may change his mind. Don't screw this up for the rest of us."

"Tell Kaleo to back down!" Samir spat the words at Kaleo. Then, with a backwards snap of his head, Samir hit the floor. Kaleo had knocked Samir square in the jaw and no one had seen it coming. We anticipated an attack of some sort but Kaleo's was so fast it caught us all off guard. Kaleo had always been fast.

Two of the Tyros went to help Samir get to his feet but their help was immediately shrugged off as Samir began to come around and he stood. He didn't want the help and he didn't make a move. The rest of us gave the two space and went to our cots to pack away the meager possessions that we had. Not a word was spoken from anyone. Kaleo and Samir watched each other for a long time. Something had happened right then and there and what it was sat just beyond my comprehension.

CHAPTER 4: TYLAN
= To Places Unknown =

When the sun crested over the horizon we were already up and in the training yard waiting for the arrival of First-Master Sanjean and his Cabal. I still had my doubts over what had happened the previous night - many of us did- and Samir was sporting a swollen eye from what happened in our room. In retrospect, Samir should be grateful that all he had was a black eye. Despite his lean built, Kaleo had a frightening power behind his hits to complement his speed. I have seen him punch holes in stone walls before and walk away with his hand intact and have even spent an hour with the physician after a spar with him. Yes, Samir was fortunate but he had stupidly barked at Tao to go away when he tried to help him to the physician. He should have went. Under the swelling something could have been broken.

I didn't realize that I had been staring at Samir until his lips curled up to a threatening sneer and Odestan nudged me on the shoulder. The door to the training yard was opening, but we did not expecting the ones who came through the door. It was a group of older Tyros, five years ahead of us in studying and on their way to becoming Masters. *Of course*, I thought, *they would be here too.* First-Master Sanjean had to be taking them with him to do the real work and taking us along to act as servants. That had to be it, and the thought started to boil my anger.

This group began to close in on us and we easily moved into a precautionary defensive stance. Here at the Masters School, unless the person approaching you was a member of your team or a close friend, it was foolish not to be watchful. Everyone was an opponent.

The men of the other Tyro were bigger and had more experience. They had already been out on scouting missions and skirmishes outside of the school to combat the strange things that nestled in the heart of the Four Kingdoms. Now they were looking at us like we were their next target, hands bereft of weapons or not.

"Shouldn't you men be about your work?" Kaleo said. His voice was low and smooth to mask the deeper accent his voice held, and his eyes were sharp as he looked at the opposing group. "There's nothing for you to see here."

That challenge was met with an eruption of grunt laughter from the men and I shifted my weight from one foot to the other.

Jayson, a man in his early twenties who was broad of shoulder and had a square jaw, stepped up to Kaleo. He towered over him by at least a foot. His body was scared by fights and some were highlighted on his fair skin. "Fledgling got some nerve telling us what to do." He stepped closer, standing toe-to-toe with Kaleo who didn't flinch or move an inch that I could see. "Now, I'm going to tell you what to do."

"Back down, or I'll put you down myself." That was Kaleo's warning. Fights happened all the time in the Masters School. People were your friends and people were your enemies, but once you were outside the Schools walls you didn't fight amongst yourselves. There was no fighting amongst the people in the Schools, it was code. Inside? Inside everything was considered training so anything was fair game.

I could feel the anger building up in the air, and almost see the intensity between Kaleo and Jayson. The older man spat in Kaleo's face. At my side Odestan left his place in line and sprang into action. "You dare----!"

Whatever else Odestan was going to say was lost when he fell to the ground, sliding back a few feet on the dirt, and curled over clutching his stomach. "Stand down, Odestan!" The words and hit had come from Kaleo. He had taken his attention off of Jayson for a moment to put down Odestan, but in that same moment Jayson stole the advantage and delivered his own blow to Kaleo's head. Then the fighting began.

We were always prepared to fight, but it only took a few passes for me to realize that my opponent wasn't pulling his punches as we were taught to do in training. Fight as if it is your life - but don't kill the other. That was the rule. I could honestly say that this guy who attacked me was trying to kill me. No time to look around and see how the others were faring, I had to survive. It was like the Tourney all over again and I was struggling to stay alive. Mouth already filling with the taste of my own blood, I hit the ground and immediately had the other mans foot crushing down on my throat. Attempting to free my neck left me wide open for a kick in the ribs and when I coughed blood sprayed from my lips.

"That's enough!" The voice boomed down from overhead on the walls. The pressure on my neck stopped but the foot remained. Everything had stopped.

My head was throbbing and my chest was burning. My vision blurred but I still attempted to turn my head to see the status of the rest of my Tyro. The only ones I saw still standing were Kaleo and Samir. I shouldn't have been surprised, and I wasn't, but they were not without their scars.

"On your feet men! Everyone, fall in line!" I recognized the voice now. It was First-Master Sanjean. He had probably been on the wall the entire time. This whole attack was probably his doing.

The guy stepped off of my neck and I rolled over in the dirt, coughing and wrapping my hands about my neck before shakily regaining my feet. The others were standing as well as they could and we retook our places in the line we had formed when we first entered the training yard this morning. While we all were suffering from whatever damages received no moans were heard in our line or theirs. I saw Jayson's arm hanging in an awkward way and knew that it was broken.

I spat at the ground to get some of the blood out of my mouth and looked up to see First-Master Sanjean coming across the yard, his Cabal following behind. Two of his members were carrying a large chest between them.

He pointed to the large wood and metal gate that lead to the world outside. "Beyond that gate is death!" The First-Master began to speak as he drew nearer. "Beyond that gate people are not going to coddle you or care about your broken bones or that you're bleeding. Beyond that gate it's you against them and if you start a fight, or someone starts one with you, you better be able to finish it!"

"Yes, First-Master Sanjean!" All of us shouted together.

He walked the line with his hands now clasped behind his back, and the two members of his Cabal that held the chest put it down on the ground and opened it. Inside were weapons. While we were not allowed to carry anything more than a dirk while we were students in the School we trained with an assortment of arms, all the better to find our mate. They said that every man had his weapon, one that was suited just for him. Personally I preferred the double-bladed longsword and hoped that there was one in the chest for me.

First-Master Sanjean continued his talk. "There are no standby physicians outside that gate. You need to fix yourself and keep going!"

He backed up and looked at the older group of Tyros and gave them a nod. "They know what it's like to look death in the face and come out victorious. Tyros!" he shouted to the others. "As you were."

That was all it took for the other group to turn and start out of the arena. Looking at the state of them I could only assume that they were going to the physicians quarters. Lucky sods. Maybe they had other training to perform and wouldn't have time to get their wounds healed.

First-Master Sanjean directed us to the chest and I went to take my pick. My sword was there, the double-bladed longsword that I had used so many times in training. Picking it up from the chest and knowing that I was going to be able to keep it - at least until we returned to the school - gave me a sense of pride. I could call the weapon mine and I strapped it on my back. A prize for my current pain.

"Kaleo," Sanjean said.

"Yes, First-Master Sanjean?" he replied while strapping on his weapons of choice. Sais. Kaleo always said he had no use of a melee weapon but the Sai was short enough for him to still engage in close range combat. It only made him deadlier.

"Get your men together, we are leaving."

"Yes, First-Master Sanjean," Kaleo responded before he turned to the rest of us. "You heard the man, wipe off your faces and let's go!"

The main gate was already opening and the two Masters that had carried the chest out to the arena closed the lid and were carrying it away. If you had not gotten your weapon by now, well, you were not getting one from that chest.

I pulled my shirt up and used it to scrub at my face. How long was it going to be before we got a chance to properly clean the blood and grit from our bodies? Before we would be able to properly tend to our wounds? I guessed it would not be until the end of the day and, as this one was just starting, that was a long way off.

Odestan caught up to me just as I was about to pass through the gate and knocked me on the shoulder. "I told you we were getting out of here," he gloated. His nose looked broken in a couple places but he was smiling. "Feels good to leave the School behind. Imagine the things we'll see out there!"

"Don't look so happy Odestan," I warned, "The Masters may make you crawl several hundred miles on your fingertips."

"Lighten up Tylan, give yourself a break for once. We're free, we made it out the School. We were chosen for this mission."

I shook my head as I regarded my friend. "Doesn't that seem just a tad suspicious to you? A fortnight ago we were Fledglings and now we're with First-Master Sanjean and his Cabal on a mission?"

Odestan scratched at the stubble on his chin. "Bet this has something to do with the war."

Before I could answer him Tao came over to us. He was shorter than I was with slanted eyes and a devious looking face. He always looked up to something. "What are you two talking about?" he inquired.

"I was telling Odestan how lucky you must feel to be out of the School," I said with a smirk upon my lips. Lying about what we really were saying. "The Fledglings can't use you for target practice anymore." Tao was broad, even with the meager portions of food we were given. He may have been big, but it was all hard muscle.

Odestan laughed at my impromptu joke and Tao punched me in the chest for my humor before he walked past us. I laughed in spite of myself and the pain and waited until he was out of ear shot before I spoke again. I still lowered my voice. "If it's about the war then why didn't they send a more experienced group huh, like the ones who attacked us? You tell me that." And I walked away from my friend.

The older Tyro groups in the school, Sachems and their Master groups, any of them could have been chosen but they hadn't. There was something else going on here and we were being left in the dark.

I turned to look back at the gate when I heard it close and when I turned back around I saw Samir watching me. The eye that was only partially swollen this morning was now completely shut. I saw malice in his gaze but didn't avert my eyes. I didn't know what his sudden problem with me was but sooner or later I was going to find out. We were outside of the school now; and things were going to be different.

##

It was six or seven hours before we stopped long enough for it to be considered a break. I felt a small amount of pity for those of us who were suffering from broken bones due to our morning scrimmage. I probably had a cracked or broken rib, but at least I didn't have to bend my ribs in order to walk. Inside the school the ground was hard packed dirt, sometimes stone, but out here it varied and there were plenty of things to trip the unwary.

The Masters School of the Iron Fist was located in the Northern Kingdom right outside Barq, the ruling city where the Governor sat. It also currently housed the King's Chair. Bordered on the south by a high mountainous range and the ocean to the east, the Kingdom was nearly cut off from the rest of the Realms, but it was defensible. It also had a lot of swampy marsh with areas of closely packed trees and surface waters. The residents had learned constructive ways of placing their houses to avoid flooding if they were not lucky enough to live in one of the sections of high ground. Barq was one of the more dangerous cities in the Realms. Wild animals were known to inhabit the marsh regions and dark creatures found their way in from over the mountains. For this reason the Iron Fist was the largest Masters School in all the Four Kingdoms and, if you asked the High-Lord Master, he would say that it produced the best men.

Reading about the outward conditions and actually traveling in them were two different things. My body felt tired and worn. Life was hard in the school but at least you had some enclosure and patted ground. A few times one of the Tyro started to fall behind, but we didn't stop. It was up to them to keep up with the rest of us. First-Master Sanjean made it clear that there was no room for the weak on this mission and if you fell behind and got lost from the group you would be labeled a deserter and that marked you for death. If you fell behind, you caught back up.

We settled down on a dry expanse of land not to far off from the main road and started gathering kindle for a fire. The Tyro didn't have much in way of supplies; the Cabal had more, two of the men even wore large packs upon their back that held the very basics in cooking supplies and bedding. I wish we had thought about what we were to do when it was time to sleep. As Masters you learned to put little value in material possessions and carry only what would not be a hinderance. We were trained to spring into action - hard to do that when you are encumbered with items. There was a creek not far from where we stopped and the members of the Tyro went down to finally properly clean themselves from the blood and grit of the morning.

The weather in the Northern Kingdom was still warm this time of year. As far north as we were it never got too cold so myself and others pulled off our shirts to give them a ringing as well. The only one not with the Tyro at the creek was Kaleo, he was sitting about the fire with First-Master Sanjean.

The fire crackled as Kaleo tossed in another dry log and began to stoke it with a stick. Right now the blaze was hardly big enough to warm one man let alone nearly twenty.

"There's distention amongst your men, Kaleo," came the observation of First-Master Sanjean. He sat a couple feet away from the younger boy and watched him even as his men were portioning out the rations. "I can feel it in the air around them."

"Samir challenged me the other night in the barracks, Sir," Kaleo responded. Sanjean didn't look very surprised. He folded his arms over his chest.

"And what did you do?"

"I knocked him out. If he wanted to be Sachem there was plenty of time for him to speak up in the arena like I did when you asked." Kaleo spoke quickly and struck hard at the fire with a stick before he tossed it into the flames. "It only took one shot."

Sanjean was quiet for a moment. "Did he retaliate?" He watched the younger man as he wanted to gauge the response to the question. He had been watching the interactions between the members of the young Tyro since they had left the school and there were some things that he did not like.

"No." came Kaleo's reply.

One of the members of the Cabal came by and brought a cup of water to the First-Master and offered one to Kaleo as well. Though he was surprised by the offer, Kaleo accepted and held the cup in is hands. He knew that he wasn't on the same level as Sanjean and he wasn't going to be so presumptuous as to drink before the other had done so first.

But Sanjean didn't drink, not right away, instead he continued to look at Kaleo and study him. "You all haven't been a Tyro for very long so let me give you some advice," Sanjean said, and he put the cup of water down on the ground in front of him. Kaleo sighed internally. He was parched and hot from being so close to the fire. The water had been very inviting. The others at the stream were likely taking in their full of water while he was sitting here with what he wanted being so close and yet so far away.

"Power can be taken away as easily as it was given." said First-Master Sanjean. "You didn't get to pick the men you have in your group, all of you earned a right to be there as much as the other. All of you have the potential to be a leader. You all have to depend upon each other to survive as a unit. There are people in your group who are better than you, stronger, have a better wit. Why should any of them listen to a sorry sod like you?"

Kaleo looked down into his cup of water. Out of the ten men of his Tyro he was the strongest of four: Samir, Odestan, Mikal and himself. Any one of those people could have challenged him for the spot, but he was the oldest of the lot.

"Age doesn't have anything to do with it," First-Master Sanjean piped in. Kaleo could have sworn the man had read his mind. "And neither does your strength. There are members of my Cabal who can take me down without even trying. You need to get your head together and figure out how to fix your Tyro before someone displaces you." Sanjean now took a drink of his water, making Kaleo free to do so as well and he nearly emptied the cup.

Kaleo stood, his thoughts were on finding his Tyro down at the lake and having a talk with them. Then another thought came to mind. He looked off in the direction he knew the creek to be and crouched down upon the ground again, attention turning back to the older man before he spoke. "First-Master Sanjean?"

"Yes...." The older man replied with a hint of irritation in his voice. He was tired and hoped that the boy wasn't about to rehash the finished conversation.

"Where are we going?" Kaleo asked. "I know we are heading west but why? What type of mission is this?"

Sanjean let out a deep sigh and then inhaled, squaring back his shoulders as he sat there and looked the Tyro leader in the eyes. "That's not information you are entitled to know."

"With respect, First-Master, you picked us for this mission and brought us out here to be a part of whatever this is. I think we are entitled to know." Kaleo's eyes were steady as he silently faced off with the First-Master. He wouldn't have dared to do that in the School and even now a small voice inside of him feared for his life.

First-Master Sanjean responded, "The Masters' Code says that the Masters are to give their might to the safety of the Four Kingdoms."

"It also says that we're not to use that might in political games." Kaleo said. They were either going to another Masters School, or to a Governor, He didn't like either option.

"Who said anything about this being political." It wasn't a question and it made Kaleo reconsider his position for a moment. The First-Master fixed Kaleo with a hard stare that bore right through him.

"If it's not political then why did you choose us to come when there are more experienced groups?" There had to be a reason behind it. The Master had said so himself that their group had problems. Did he really think that they could accomplish whatever it was that needed to be done if they still had to work on themselves? It could be some game to show the other schools, and Kingdoms, what the Iron Fist could do with unseasoned boys.

The right corners of Sanjean's lips curled up into a coy smile. "Why indeed." That was all that he said and the First-Master turned away from Kaleo and went back to his water and the fire.

It was frustrating to not get an answer and pressing further for one wouldn't get any results. Kaleo sucked his teeth and muttered under his breath. He left, leaving is cup where he had been sitting at the fire.

Sanjean had a look of satisfaction on his face as he watched the young Tyro leave. *A hot headed sod that boy is.*

Alyn, a member of the Cabal, walked up and stood besides his leader. "That boy is blindsided by his own ambition. Do you think he'll figure it out?" Alyn asked.

Sanjean considered this before he answered. "He might. But when he does it may already be to late. Let's eat, we have spent enough time here."

##

Our late lunch came and went and all to soon we were back on the road. We were clean, though some of us still wet from the creek, and we had tended to our injuries the best we could without medical supplies. I wished we had stayed longer as the whole experience was wearing on my damaged body and I found myself wishing time would go faster so that we could settle down for the night. A full rest would be just what my body needed - that and more than a poor ration of food - but it wouldn't be night for a few more hours yet.

The people we came across on the road stepped wide around to give us room. We were nearing the village that sat near the base of the mountain. It was interesting to see peoples reactions. From their expressions you would have thought we looked like monsters the way mothers pulled their children away and how people were so quick to avert their eyes. Something was wrong here. The Masters were an esteemed group. Parents were proud, honored even, to have their son selected to enter a School, so why did these people seem so afraid?

Word of our coming preceded us for as we arrived at that village, an hour or two later, we found the people had holed themselves up inside of their homes. First-Master Sanjean brought us to a stop near the center of the village and spoke in low tones to the members of his Cabal so we wouldn't over hear what was being said.

"I have a funny feeling about this place." Chulin said, looking around.

"You have a funny feeling about everything." Mikal answered. They were standing next to each other just ahead of me.

Chulin shook his head. "Don't downplay my feelings, I've learned to trust my gut."

"Pfft, must be why you still have it." Mikal joked.

I took a few steps forward to get into the conversation Chulin and Mikal were having. "What are you two talking about?" I asked.

"Chulin's hungry," mused Mikal.

"I am hungry, but that's not what's at question," Chulin said. I always found it odd that Chulin was even in the school. I've known him for about as long as the other guys but, unless he was engaged in combat the man was slightly clumsy and a bit odd. "I've got a funny feeling about this place."

"It is odd, isn't it? How the people have been responding to us." I stated.

Mikal grunted and waved his hand in dismissal. "Not you too, Tylan. There's nothing wrong here. These people are only giving us the respect that we deserve by getting out of our way."

"They are scared, Mikal," I said in challenge to his words. "People are not suppose to be afraid of their proctors." Something had to have happened here.

Doors of one of the storehouses opened up and out came a few older male villagers carrying hoes, pitchforks and other various farming tools as weapons. "You all need to keep passing through. We've had enough of your kind around here." That was spoken by the grey bearded man holding a scythe. Despite his age, the man didn't look feeble. His skin darkened and leathery from years of working the stubborn land to produce results, but he looked as hardened as one of the men in the Cabal.

His hands that worked the handle of the harvest tool moved with experience and the man took a challenging step towards First-Master Sanjean. The Cabal responded to the challenge by moving up and formed a standing line.

"Leave our village," the man said, "Or we'll make you leave."

CHAPTER 5 : SCOTIA
= An Unlikely Refuge =

Maerilea and I ran. We ran as long and as fast as we could. Our bodies were tired and worn from not being use to such exertion. Driven by adrenaline and fear we didn't stop until we finally collapsed in a collection of bushes a couple miles from Ravensbro.

"My legs. I can't, I can't run anymore," Maerilea managed to say as she worked hard at catching her breath. I was in no better condition as I laid upon the ground coughing while trying to remain as quiet as I could.

"What were the Masters doing?" Maerilea asked. Good, she had noticed what they were as well. "Why were they there? How....far...did we get?" So many questions and I couldn't think of an answer to any of them. My throat was burning and my legs starting to grow numb.

Through the haze that was cast over my eyes I looked back from where we came. We had put a lot of distance between ourselves and Ravensbro but I could still smell the smoke and see the sky alight with fire. The sound of screams continued to echo in my head, a woefully lullaby as I passed out on the ground.

##

The prosperous trade city of Ravensbro was aflame. Buildings were burning and there were dead bodies everywhere. The people that didn't manage to escape the city and who survived, were corralled to an open section of the city by the large black hooded men. There was a general sense of fear amongst the people as they were separated, collared, and put into caged wagons. Onto the scene came two broad shouldered men with weapons strapped on their backs. The way that they walked and the crest worn on their belts marked them as Masters too and the people who saw them knew who they were. There was a spark of hope amongst the prisoners as they thought the men were there to help. Maybe, just maybe, these were the good guys and not the pretenders who had destroyed their home.

The people started calling out to the Masters for help, extending their arms through the cages and rattling their chains.

Some of them even tried to fight against their captors to no avail. The hooded men saw the new arrivals as well but didn't stop in their task.

One of the Masters, whom was broad and bore a patch over his left eye, walked over to the closest wagon, a smug look on his face. "Thank the Heavens you're here. Please, help us," begged an older woman, relief tinging on her voice as shaky hands reached out to touch him.

Before she could make contact with him the Master grabbed her hand and pulled her hard against the cool iron bars. She cried out in pain and fear, her face pressed against the bars. The sudden and surprising action made the others in the wagon move as far back as they could from the Master.

The Master held the woman's hand firmly in his grasp, nearly crushing her fingers and kept her tight against the bars. He watched in satisfaction as the fear in her eyes grew. "Why would I help you?" The Master hissed.

The woman's eyes teared, the water streaked down her dirty face. A near silent plea passed over her lips. "Don't do this." The answer was not forthcoming. Instead the Master eased her back in the cage then yanked harshly on her arm, pulling the woman forward once again. Her head slammed against the rails and she passed out. He let her hand go and she fell the rest of the way to the wagon floor. Cries and wailings followed the Master as he left the cage.

"Hurry it up you worthless packs of grit!" The Master yelled out to the hooded men who were rounding up the people. "We have a schedule to keep." He muttered to himself before he met up with the other man who had come with him.

##

I was not sure how long I had been out, but when I awoke I was startled to see that I was lying in a covered straw bed and dressed in only my shift. Maerilea dozed in a seat at my side. It looked like we were in a small room of someones home. I didn't know how we got here. In the dim light of the room I saw that my left arm was bandaged though I didn't remember it being tended either. All I could remember were the bushes and the fire.

"Mother...." I whispered as I clenched the thin light blue sheet I was under. Just then the door opened and more light flooded into the room followed by a portly woman who was carrying a tray.

"Oh good, you're awake," the woman said, a relieved smile stretching across her kind face. She was dressed rather plainly in an old brown tunic and skirt that reached to the floor. As she got closer with the tray I gave hard nudges to my friend until she finally woke up. She didn't seem as shocked as I had and sat up slowly.

"Oh, Scotia, you're awake." Maerilea yawned with a stretch.

The woman placed the tray on the side table, it had a simple pot, a couple cups and a block of cheese and bread. "Your friend was starting to worry." She said.

"What do you mean?" I asked. I couldn't have been that injured to cause worry. I had only fallen asleep.

"You've been asleep for two days ---" The old lady said as she poured cups of tea.

I shot forward in the bed. "Two days!" That can't be right.

"You had me really worried," Maerilea put her arms around my shoulders and drew me in for a hug. Two days? I couldn't believe what they were saying.

"I found the two of you unconscious and lying in the bushes a little ways outside of Ravensbro. I was going there to complete my weekly trade and was surprised at what I saw; figured the two of you were survivors." The lady explained. "I have never seen the city like that before. Ravaged. There was barely anything left."

"Did you find anyone else?" I asked, thinking about my mother. After seeing the blood and carnage of the Tavern I assumed our coachman and footman to be dead but, perhaps my mother had made it.

Maerilea began to stroke my hair, holding me closer to her. Though I didn't hear anything I could feel her sigh. Neither answered my question so I turned to get a look at my friends face. Her expression was solemn and at the moment I had wanted to take back my question. Still, I wanted to know. People had been running out of the city, surely there had to be some survivors or people who had traveled back to see what they could salvage.

"There isn't anything there, Scotia," said Maerilea softly. "Only dead bodies and whatever hasn't been eaten by the birds and wild animals. The city is in ruins."

"I will just leave the two of you alone," interjected the woman as she started towards the door. "Breakfast will be ready shortly. Maerilea, dear, help your friend adjust."

"Yes, Phyllis, of course. Thank you." Maerilea said before the woman left out the door and the two of them alone in the room. Maerilea released me from her arms only to keep a hand on my shoulder. "Scotia, there's something evil resting over that city. I can't explain to you what it is, but I know it's not right. The Kenisis around that place is very unsettling. We should go back to the Order and report this."

I shook my head. "No. No we can't go back to the Order. What about mother? What about Certima? We're suppose to go to Certima." *Go to Certima as fast as you can, that had been what mother told us to do. To go to Certima.*

"That was before all of this happened. You can't be seriously considering still going there are you? Remember why she said we were going to Certima in the first place? We were being given to Governor Rycliff. Do you really want to be a slave that badly that you're willing to go there yourself!" Maerilea looked shocked and appalled. "The Ma'Tradom is dead. We need to look out for ourselves."

"By going back to the Order when they think we're going to Certima? Did you forget about the way they treated us back there? What makes you think we'd even be welcomed?" I pushed away from her and placed my feet on the floor and stood. I felt hungry, ravenous, and headed over to where Phyllis had left the tray and ate into half of the bread.

"If we go back to the Order all they will do is send us back," I spoke around the food that was in my mouth. "And, if going back there was such a good idea, don't you think she would have told us to go there instead of continuing on to our planned destination?" It was odd how mother had been insistent on us going to the city - which was further away - and not back to the Order.

"It's cold in here. Where are my clothes?" Unsure if the cold was from lack of warmth or worry I still wanted to feel something more around me than a shift. Maerilea went to the end of the bed and opened the top of a chest that sat at the foot of it on the floor. "They're in here. I think that if we go back to the Order and explain to them what happened they'll realize why we returned."

I found my clothing in the chest like Maerilea said and dressed. "You can go back to the Order if you want, Maerilea, but I'm going to Certima. It's not because I want to be a slave, but Ma'Tradom had to have good reason for sending us to city. Don't you see? 'There are certain things that must be done.'" to quote the words of my mother and ones that the Order lived by.

I looked in the chest for my Proxi cloak and couldn't find it. "Maerilea? Where are our cloaks?"

"They're in the chest, aren't they?"

I bent down to get a better look into the chest, moving around the blankets that were inside just in case the cloaks happened to be under them, but I still could not find them. When the carriage had pulled up outside of the Inn mother had said to stay close and not to talk to anyone. I didn't ask what that meant then, I should have, and now it had me wondering. "What do you suppose mother meant when she told us not to talk to anyone?"

"Likely that she thought we were going to try an escape." Answered Maerilea.

"I'm being serious Maerilea, what have you told Phyllis?" Perhaps I was being paranoid, but I gave a hard look at the plate of food and then crept to the door to peer out. "You don't find it a little bit suspicious that she just happened to find us?"

"Give it a break, Scotia! People see people on the side of roads all the time." Maerilea said, annoyance showing through in her tone.

"We were in the bushes!" I stated. I didn't remember much, but I remembered that the bushes kept us from easy sight.

Maerilea got up and approached me, pulling on my hand to show the bandaged arm. "Phyllis has been nothing but kind since she found us, she even patched up your arm that you cut in the bushes. She got us back to health after the fire and provided us with shelter. She's not our enemy."

Phyllis' voice came from the next room. "Girls! Breakfast!"

I opened my mouth to say something but Maerilea held up her hand and I swallowed my words. I didn't know anything about our host, my friend who had been awake for days did. Or she thought that she did, and I owed her the benefit of a doubt on this. At least for now. So I held my tongue and moved away from the door and we exited out for breakfast.

It was a simple fare of fresh biscuits, meat, and fruit - the last taking me by surprise.

"Don't often get fruit like this around here this time of year," I said in a slight observation while I ate.

Phyllis was ever bright and cherry. Her smile never faltered, it was quite eerie. "Imported. All the way from the Lands Across the Sea." Phyllis said proudly. For a person who imported goods she lived in quaint accommodations. It was a small house with a main room, bedroom and a washroom. Where did she get the money?

"Imported?" I asked. The trading port at Ravensbro only brought in fruit on rare occasions, the main trading there were material goods and slaves. These fruits would have had to come a long way which would have made them all the more expensive to buy.

"Thank you, Phyllis, for putting us up," I said, trying to disregard the strange feeling that I had. But something wasn't right here. "We would not want to impose on you more than we have. My friend and I should get going after breakfast."

Phyllis' cheery expression tightened. "Whats the rush?" She asked. "You only just woke up, Scotia. You need to rest a day or two and build up your strength. Besides, I could use two girls like you. Help me out around the place."

"She's right, Scotia," Maerilea said, staring me down. "You should rest a bit and helping out is the least that we can do to repay her kindness."

I was faced with a choice about what could I do. If I left now I knew that my friend wouldn't come with me. I wanted her to follow me to Certima so we could figure out what was going on; and I didn't want to be alone. I looked at Maerilea then Phyllis, and back again to my friend before I lowered my eyes and nodded.

"Yes. Yes you're right," I said softly and rose from my seat. "Please excuse me, I'm feeling tired." As I turned to head back into the room I could swear that Phyllis had a look of satisfaction on her face.

##

We stayed with Phyllis for the rest of that day and a couple days after. Since I was here I decided to use it as an opportunity to learn more about our host. I admit she wasn't a bad person, I only didn't trust her. Maybe it was because she smiled a lot, or it was because every time I made mention of leaving she would be quick to change the subject. Not to mention that I still hadn't found our cloaks.

I still wanted to work on my Kinesis, but Phyllis always kept me in her sights and I didn't want her to see my weaknesses or know that we came from the Order. I hoped Maerilea hadn't told her. I couldn't help but think she was watching us.

Helping out with chores around the house wasn't foreign as we did work like this all the time in the Order and it was an opportunity to look around the small abode discreetly. There was no farm outside and she had no animals, not even a horse. How then did she manage to bring both Maerilea and myself here to her house from the city? At the start of our fourth day with Phyllis I found something, and it sealed my conviction that my friend and I had to leave the house as soon as we could.

Hidden in a small hovel at the back of the house was an herbal garden. I found it after I had tripped over a rock and fell on the ground. It was well masked with small planks of wood that leaned against the house. Moving the wood I saw a green and red leaf plant growing out of the dirt. I wasn't the best in Geo, but even though I didn't know what I was looking at I could feel the Kenisis it produced and it felt wrong. I sniffed at the herb and was surprised to discover it smelled exactly like the tea Phyllis made for us every day. Wetting my lips I looked around to make sure Phyllis wasn't near, I put my hands into the dirt and uprooted one of the plants and stuffed it in my skirt pocket. *If I show this to Maerilea, she'll have to believe me. Then we can get out of here.* The sound of horse hooves upon the ground startled me. I hadn't heard sounds of anyone coming around since we got here. Someone was coming to the house.

Making my way to the front I saw him, a broad shoulder man of darkened skin. He wore a heavy leather breastplate and a sheathed weapon on his back. I would have placed him as merely a mercenary or a guard, but I then I saw the crest he wore upon his belt. He was a Master. They weren't known for traveling alone - there were two of them at least - so why was this one alone and why was he here? After those Masters had attacked us in Ravensbro his presence here make me feel uneasy.

I watched as the Master tethered his horse on the front porch rail and then knocked on the door. "Come in!" I heard Phyllis call from inside the house. She must have been expecting him, otherwise I thought that she would have asked to see who was paying a visit. She couldn't have thought it was me, else I would have gone in without knocking.

This was the perfect opportunity to make an escape. Where was Maerilea? Of course, she was inside helping Phyllis prepare supper. Oh Maerilea, why couldn't you have been out here with me? We could have stollen the horse and rode away from here. I did not even know if she was going to come with me or still insist on going back to the Order as we hadn't the time to speak on it more. But I had the herb in my pocket. I'd be able to convince her to come with me. If I went in to get my friend I had to have faith that we would be able to get back out again.

There was a window on the side of the house and I peered inside. Phyllis and the Master were sitting down at the table and there was Maerilea, smiling and serving up a pot of tea. Things couldn't be bad if she was smiling. Drawing in a deep breath I picked up my chin and entered through the front door. There was something I was suppose to say to the Master, a greeting, but I could not think of it at the moment so instead I only bowed my head as I saw the Master was looking at me. "I saw a horse outside." That was the only thing I could think of to say as I stood there inside the door.

"Don't be shy now, Scotia. Come in and sit with us after you have put the wood by the fire." Phyllis said.

The wood? Oh, I had forgotten the wood. That's what I was suppose to be collecting at the back of the house. I looked at Maerilea and we locked eyes for a moment before I looked to Phyllis. "In the shock of the guests' arrival I forgot. I'll go and get it." Taking this as my chance for a getaway I turned, ready to leave out the door.

"That won't be necessary," the Master said with a deep voice. His words caused me to stop my actions, fingers partially curled around the doorknob. He stood up from the table and made a single brush of his hands down his breastplate. "As the girl said, it's my fault she forgot the wood."

"N-no that's not what I said," it was an effort to keep my voice from shaking, but he was now standing in front of me and I felt small and weak. The Master was so close to me that I could make out his features in fine detail. There was simply something about him that terrified and fascinated me at the same time.

The Master nodded and reached for the knob, which I was quick to surrender and move away from him. For a moment I thought that he was going to open the door and let me out, I hoped this was true. "That is what you said. Sit down," said the Master. It wasn't a question and I moved from the door and obediently sat down next to my friend. If he had been a female I feel that I wouldn't have given up so easily. But I had, and now my chances of going out and leaving on the horse were bleak. He left out the door instead.

No one said anything but Phyllis continued to smile as she always did and it only grew when the Master returned carrying logs of firewood in his arms. I watched as he put the stack by the fireplace and then put one into the fire. With the task done he returned to his seat and as he was doing so Phyllis spoke. "Girls, this is Master Naethin of the Eagle's Claw, the Masters School in Certima."

Certima? I perked up when I heard what she said. He's from Certima? It had to be more than coincidence that he was from the very place that we were told to go. Maybe he was even sent here to find us for Governor Rycliff and take us there.

"They heard about what happened a few miles down in Ravensbro," said Phyllis.

"I never expected Phyllis to find girls like you in a city like that," said Master Naethin. "She says you're from Arameyth."

"Yes, Sir." Maerilea responded.

She seemed willing to give information. I hadn't noticed that tea had been poured and cups were at each of our places. Maerilea was drinking hers. Thinking of the tea I thought about the plant in my pocket. I didn't know what it was but it was in the tea and I wasn't going to drink it. How many times have we been served tea?

"What was your purpose in Ravensbro?" Naethin's voice was low and direct, his eyes looking straight at Maerilea.

Just as she opened her mouth to answer I gave her a quick kick to the shin with my foot under the table. Instead of words she jumped with a yelp. "Scotia! What in the blazes is your problem!" Bending down she rubbed the sore spot on her leg.

"I thought I felt a mouse run across my foot." I lied. Phyllis was looking at me with that never ending smile of hers but I choose to look at my friend instead, even placing a hand on her shoulder. "I'm sorry."

"Here," said Phyllis, picking up the tea kettle and refilling Maerilea's cup. "Have some more tea. Scotia, you haven't touched yours."

"I'm not thirsty, thank you." Actually I was, but I wasn't willing to trust the tea after what I found outside and seeing the way that my friend was acting.

There was a pause of silence after that before the Master spoke again in his low tones. "It's rare for girls like yourself to travel alone. Who else was with you? Perhaps I have seen them on my way here."

"We didn't travel alone, we have each other." I said.

The Master got up and went to a chest that Phyllis kept in the kitchen. It had always been locked before, but Master Naethin took a key out of his pant pocket and unlocked the chest. "Arameyth. The Order is located in that city, is it not?" He asked.

I was nervous. Neither Maerilea nor I answered. I kept watching him as he reached inside the chest and dug around. "Two young girls traveling alone. You wouldn't happen to be from the Order would you?"

We did not have the bracelets girls received when they reached Proxi, and we didn't have our cloaks. There was nothing to mark us as anything besides ordinary females. Phyllis had our cloaks somewhere. I knew she did.

"Powerful women." Maerilea said in a sleepy voice. I couldn't hide the shock on my face as I looked at her, but it only lasted a moment and I looked back to see Phyllis' wide smiling face staring at me and Naethin pull something from out of the chest.

He had in his hand our Proxi cloaks. I knew we hadn't left them, and now there they were in the Master's hand. I was afraid. My mother's warning of not talking to anyone spoke out loud in my head. I was afraid and couldn't breath.

"Then these would be yours." Master Naethin said.

Maerilea's eyes lit up as she looked at our cloaks hanging in Naethin's hands. "My cloak! You found it!"

"Maerilea!" I reached for her as she stood up and grabbed her around the waist to pull her back. "What do you want with us? And what have you done to Maerilea!" I demanded to know. She was intoxicated. Phyllis was standing now as well, her hands folded down in front of her. Naethin came closer, our cloaks wrapped in his arms.

"Scotia, you haven't been drinking your tea." Phyllis, even now, had that smile fixed on her face. Thanks to her I may never drink tea again.

I held on to Maerilea, she was tugging against me to get to her cloak. "I don't want any tea!" I shouted to Phyllis. "Maerilea trusted you! We thought you were our friend!"

"I am helping you, dear," Phyllis claimed, her voice cheery and light. "Master Naethin is here to help you, too."

"I don't believe you!" I said in retort.

"Whether you do or not, both of you are coming with me." The Master said. Outside of the cottage came the rattling of a carriage. Someone else was here. He looked to the door. "It's time to go." He began to approach.

"Scotia, look. You were right." Maerilea stopped pulling against me and was wobbly on her feet. Instead of holding her back I was now holding her up. "We did bring our cloaks. Now we can go home." What was in that tea? It was served at every meal here but Maerilea had never acted like this.

There was nowhere for me to go. I could try to run past the Master and out the door, but that would be hard to do while holding my friend. Instead I dragged her backwards with me. "Maerilea. Maerilea snap out of it!" I needed her to come to herself. She was better skilled in the use of Kenisis and maybe she could do something to help us. Naethin was converging on us and I held on tighter to my friend. "Snap out of it! Help me!" I yelled to her, holding even tighter and burring my head into her back. "Help me Maerilea!"

Something happened then. The fireplace erupted and I was thrown against the wall and lost my hold on Maerilea. I hit my head, the cottage was ablaze and then I loss consciousness.

CHAPTER 6: TYLAN
= Rumors =

Something was defiantly wrong here. Citizens were threatening to fight against Masters. The thought was absurd. Why would they do such a thing? More importantly, why would First-Master Sanjean and his Cabal look at this seriously? They couldn't really be considering fighting these people. Yet they had taken on a battle ready stance, as had the rest of the Tyro.

"Are you all deaf! I told you to leave out before we force you out!" Shouted the older man and he backed up his threat by taking a couple forward steps and slicing the air with his scythe. The way he handled the large tool showed experience and skill that could have only come from years of use - or intense training.

For few moments no one moved and nothing was said, then Sanjean stepped forward and spread his hands out in a small gesture of peace. Perhaps it was more of a mockery. "You must have lost hold of your senses, old man, to address us as such."

"It's more than you deserve!" Came a shout from someone else in the crowd followed by accompanying shouts of: thieves, slavers, lecherous beast, and other names that were being yelled from the villagers.

I felt my chest tighten and fist curl up at my side. Samir rested his hand on the hilt of his weapon that sat on the side of his hip. Kaleo must have seen it too as he reached a hand back to Samir, signaling him to hold his position.

I couldn't blame Samir for being angry. How dare these people say such things about the Masters! Men who fought hard to save such people like these from things they couldn't even imagine! Despite his stance First-Master Sanjean remained calm, as did the others in his team. When he spoke it was loud enough to be heard above the din of the crowd. "We are not the barbaric men you make us out to be. True Masters would not exhibit such behavior to cause such a stir."

Clearly the people had been expecting the Masters to retaliate in a physical manner instead of a verbal one. There was a sense of confusion amongst the people as they heard what First-Master Sanjean said and the way we were holding ourselves. It was likely different than what they had experienced to make them think so poorly of us. Even so, none of them lowered their weapons nor did they back down. Except the old man. His hands didn't relax their hold but I did noticed an ease of the tension in his shoulders.

"A few nights ago Masters, men like you, attacked our village," the older man started to explain. "We knew who they were and welcomed them at first. Gave them food and rest. They were particularly interested in our children, not just the young men, but the women too. They took the oldest children from us!" There was a lot of heat behind his words. "We lost a lot of good men in our attempt to fight back before they finally left. The Masters said that they would be back in a few days. The time has passed and now you show up. I'll be damned if we let you take anything else from us!" As the man spoke the tension in his body returned. The pain of his tale was written all over his face and he was filled with a renewed vigor.

I could barely remember my sister - and I had an even foggier memory of my mother. The guys in the School were the only family I knew. We fought and bleed together through our trails. It was hard for me to understand the loss the old man must have been feeling. Though the anger, the anger I knew.

My first thought was that whoever these people were, they were not real Masters but impersonators. This theory was quickly put down. "There have been rumors about a group of Masters that have turned against the code," said First-Master Sanjean.

I was shocked and surprised at what I heard. The Code of the Masters was beaten into each and every one of us at the School starting the day we arrived. Number one: never get involved in political games. Number two: don't fight each other without just cause. Number three: protect the weak (which to us meant everyone who wasn't us). Number four: give your might to the good of the Realms. The last was often confused with the first rule as doing what was good for the Realms could be seen as aiding a persons political agenda.

"They will be hunted down and brought to heel," said the First-Master. We all knew he was really saying that the men would be found and killed. You did not break the code. He turned to face his Cabal and motioned them close to him and they talked in low tones. Seeing this the people of the town relaxed, a few of them even put down their weapons.

The Tyro and the Cabal relaxed, though Samir went from one type of anger to another. Now, instead of being upset over what we were called, he was upset that there was to be no fighting.

The day was quickly getting behind us and we would need to bunker down for the night soon, but none of us were going to go anywhere until we were told.

First-Master Sanjean finished talking to his Cabal and addressed the old man since he was the one talking for the village. "My men and I will set up a perimeter around your village and make sure you're safe for the night, but only if you let down your guard and let us make camp. We've traveled a long way and require rest and food."

First-Master Sanjean was doing the right thing by getting the man to say that us being here was alright. Even though it was not needed, he was showing the man respect and trying to restore some of the Masters' credibility. We could not have people being afraid of the Masters, plus we didn't need rumors of that type attached to us.

The older man looked at Sanjean for a moment and then, finally, he put down his weapon. The scythes blade touched the ground, though the handle was still in his hand. One by one the rest of the villagers followed suit. The two groups had come to an accord and all of us could now rest a bit easier.

##

As I went about helping to set up of our camp I still sensed unease from the people. They smiled politely at us but they kept their distance, especially the females. Before leaving the school the only female contact I had was when I had received my branding as a Tyro and the Ma'Tradom held my arm. Since then it had only been in passing on the road. Here I was actually able to look at one for more than a moment and some of them gave me feelings that I didn't understand. Whenever I watched a female for too long she quickly turned away and left. I couldn't blame them. The others who had come here had treated them badly, it was only natural to be afraid.

The older man who had addressed us was named Tomas and he was the Elder of the village. I didn't know much about the Elders, our text didn't tell much aside from the fact that the Elders were appointed by the Kingdom's Governor and were said to be men of special ability. Whether it was true or not - some thought it only to be a superstition - their appointments were hardly questioned. Normally these people were only found in cities as they held a large population of people, so for this tiny village to have any marked it as unique. Maybe there was some truth to the myth about the Elders and that is why this place had been the target of the attack.

It came as no surprise when Kaleo came to me later that day and said that the Tyro had been giving first and second watch over the village. We were new, of course we would get the most shifts. We were put into pairs: I was with Odestan, Mikal with Chulin, Tao paired with Antone, Raft was with Gabriel, and surprisingly Kaleo was teaming up with Samir. With a small satchel of food and water my partner and I headed to our post along the West quadrant of the village.

Odestan and I worked well together - we weren't afraid to give the other a good punch in the face in order to bring us back to reality. "Why do you always look like you got a lot on your mind, Tylan? If you don't learn to relax your face every once in a while and smile you'll wear that scowl forever. You'll never get a girl to look twice at you," Odestan said.

"What do you know about girls and what they like? You've had about as much contact with them outside the school as me." I commented, shrugging my shoulder. "None of the females here will look at me for more than a few seconds. Besides, we have more important things to think about like that group of Masters that passed through here."

"That's exactly the reason why you should think about the girls," said Odestan. "You're always so serious, you are going to die before you get any joy out of this life." I looked away from him and rolled my eyes. "Did you ever think that if you stop being so serious all the time you'll be able to think better?"

It was hard for me to relax. The majority of the boys came into the school at ten years of age, I was brought into the Masters School when I was eight years old and have had to fight my way every since with guys who were sometimes twice my age. I didn't know what it meant to really relax. I met Odestan when I was nine, he was a year older than me and had come to the school with a positive disposition that even the whips couldn't get out of him. Positive, not cheery. I don't believe anyone at the School was ever cheery.

"Then you tell me why Masters would do something like this, huh? The Code's been beaten into me such that it's in my blood, going against it would probably kill me." I said, looking at him and wanting answers even if he had none to give.

Odestan didn't say anything for a moment. He stood there biting the bottom of his lip and cast a look around him making sure that there was no one around. There wasn't. We had walked outside of the village for our patrol and could see anything within the perimeter of our light. Then he lowered his voice and leaned closer to me and whispered, "I eavesdropped on First-Master Sanjean when he was talking to his Cabal."

"You what!" I couldn't believe what he said.

"Ssh!" He waved his hands and looked around once more. "Keep it down! Look they didn't see me." So he thought. "And even if they did, no one has said anything so you don't either. What matters is that I heard them talking about that rouge group. This isn't the first village that they've ravaged. Apparently things like this have been happening in cities all over the Four Kingdoms with different groups and they all have been taking prisoners."

"Are you telling me that we're out here hunting down Masters?" What Odestan said was insane. We couldn't fight Masters, especially not ones who have been marked for years. They would kill us without a thought. "Why were they taking prisoners?" Masters often would go out to the cities to recruit young men, but they never took prisoners - let alone female prisoners. A person couldn't be forced to be in a Masters School - you were even allowed to leave before you reached Fledgling if it was something you truly wished (though I have never seen anyone leave once they were in). After that you could only be free of the school after reaching the Master rank and by then your life was the school and the Code.

"As you said, the Code is in our blood, none of us can easily turn our back on it. I think that dark forces are at work here and the Schools are being used as pawns because of our strength."

What Odestan said made sense to me and I told him so as I clamped my hand down on his shoulder. If there were people like the women of the Order and the Elders - if it could be believed - with powers, then why couldn't there be someone causing ill? We already knew of the things that creeped about in the darkened shadows, the unnatural beast that walked the lands. Why couldn't the beast be a person? My face scrunched up tighter than before. Odestan was right, my face was probably going to get stuck that way.

PAST'S PROLOGUE

I sighed as I looked around us, hearing grass crunch and twigs snap under my feet every few steps that I took. Taking the first two shifts was not the problem - I had many sleepless nights at the school - but now Odestan had filled my head with a bunch of other things to think about. We had hours left to go and my focus wasn't as it should.

The wind blew cold and I shivered. The simple clothing I wore was not going to be enough for the upcoming climate of the mountains or the change of seasons. Coming from the North our clothing was generally light since our temperatures were not cold and to keep us from getting dehydrated in the harsh heat of summer. We were going to have to buy new clothing to prevent ourselves from getting ill as we continued.

"If someone is targeting Masters then we better keep our guard up for our own sakes." I said to him, and then the conversation lulled. We took a break from patrol and sat back down at our fire to warm up. The wind picked up again, only this time harder and it whipped under the simple belted tunic that I wore and pulled at my hair. I tossed a few more logs into the hearth. Sparks flew up and I thought that I caught the shadow of something in the distance waiting just outside the fire's light. It was midnight, the start of our second shift, and I was already feeling tired. What I saw was probably nothing at all but my imagination. Still, I squinted my eyes in that direction to try and get a better view. I saw nothing. I don't know if Odestan saw it, but the way he was scanning the night as he chewed on a strip of rawhide marked him just as uneasy.

The night became eerily silent. A few moments ago there had been sounds of nighttime creatures making their way in the dark, foliage moving with the wind and even the whisper of water in the nearby creek. Now there was nothing. Even the fire had lost its crackle. Loosening my double-sided sword from its sheath I rose slowly from the ground. Odestan was up too, his crescent axe at the ready in his hands. "Something is out there," he said quietly and began to ease his way to the edge of the firelight.

I picked up one of the logs that was sticking out of the fire and brought it along as a torch. Odestan took the lead as I checked our back and sides while still trying to pierce through the night and see if anything was there. I stayed a few steps behind my partner and we both walked quietly past the boundary of our post. This area was dense with trees and heavy foliage - the nearby creek is to thank for that. Using the light we checked the ground for prints. Right inside a small line of trees Odestan saw half of a footprint pressed into the dirt. We followed its direction and were rewarded with the same set of prints leading further into the trees.

"These prints are fresh," Odestan stated in low tones, crouching down to the ground to get a better look. "I'd say they were not more than an hour old."

"But how can that be?" I asked. Even whispering as we were our voices sounded loud in the absence of any other sound around us. "We came this way twice. We would have seen something." *So I had seen something, but that was only moments ago. Maybe they have been watching us?* It was an unnerving thought.

We continued on a bit more cautiously than before. Moving further down we heard something and saw a shadow pass not to far from where we were. The shadow belonged to a tall man in a black cloak. I couldn't even be sure it was a man for both the figure and the cloak were nearly as dark as the night itself. I would have missed him all together if I hadn't been looking so intently into the darkness. If he was the one whom I saw when I put the logs in the fire then it was no wonder that I had doubted my own eyes. Now that I saw him I kept him in my sight. He was traveling through the trees, walking at a sure and steady pace away from the village. He didn't get far when I saw a patch of night move not far from him. It was another one.

"Put out the torch!" Odestan whispered quickly, and I complied. Though it was now harder to see, we didn't want to welcome a fight unprepared.

Another moving shadow appeared, then another. It was always a surprise when I realized that another had joined as I swore there was nothing there before but darkness. One moment they were there, then suddenly they were gone. Disappeared or I lost them in the darkness. I was staring so intently that Odestan startled me when he nudged me on the side.

"Come on. We need to report this to First-Master Sanjean," said Odestan in a whisper before he started to return to the village.

"Tell him what? I don't even know what we saw," I muttered back. He wanted to report shadows? At least I knew that Odestan had seen them too and my eyes were not playing tricks on me. Neither of us said anything on the way back. Without the light from the torch our progress was slow. I didn't mind. After what I saw I was wary of any shadows in the forest.

When we arrived back to our post Kaleo was pacing in front of our fire. When we came into view his spacing stopped. "Where the devil have the two of you sods been? You're not suppose to leave your post without warning!" Kaleo was furious.

"We saw something in the woods." said Odestan.

"Men who came out of the shadows. Who were shadows." I added. "We followed a set of tracks into the forest."

Kaleo tightened his jaw and looked at us with skeptical eyes. "Are you sure about this?" He had no reason to doubt us and yet our story about walking shadows was questionable.

"One of those things was right outside our fire's light, watching us." I said. "We have to tell the First-Master."

We didn't have to go looking for him. When Kaleo didn't find us at our post he had reported it to Sanjean and they were coming to find us.

Sanjean arrived with a few members of his Cabal and looked at the three of us, though when he spoke he only addressed one of us. "Kaleo, what's going on here?" he asked in a no nonsense tone.

The Sanchem was always addressed. It didn't matter if they were part of what was going on or not, they were in charge of the group and therefore it was their responsibility to know and give a proper response. There have been times on this trip that I envied the attention that Kaleo received from the First-Master as I hated being overlooked, but this was not one of them.

"Tylan and Odestan saw men who were made of the shadows, Sir," Kaleo explained. "They followed a trail of their footprints into the trees."

When it was said like that it didn't sound very believable. Tomas had said it was Masters that had attacked their village, not walking shadows. If I hadn't seen it for myself I would have thought it all to be a lie. Whether he believed us or not I couldn't tell for it was hard to read the expression on Sanjean's face. After a moment he nodded and then pushed past us, heading towards the trees. "Bring a torch," he commanded. "Let's find these footprints."

I looked down at my shoes an took a glance to Odestan, hopefully we had not marred the trail in getting back to the village. If First-Master Sanjean saw nothing there would be no proof to our story and I didn't want to think of what would happen.

We followed behind him and Kaleo took a torch from one of the men and held it low to the ground. The easiest of tracks to see belonged to Odestan and myself, I started to think that perhaps he and I had both been seeing things due to fatigue and the cold but then the First-Master found a track about 40 feet away from where Odestan had found the first one. He turned around and walked back to the men who were waiting by our post.

"Alyn, wake up the rest of the Cabal and have them stand watch with the Tyro, we're going to see what this is about." Alyn nodded in response and went to carry out the order as Kaleo, Odestan and I followed First-Master Sanjean deeper into the trees.

We went slower this time and were on full alert for anything that may be out there. If these things could come out of the darkness there was no telling where they could be and daylight was still hours away. The cold feeling came over me again and my skin crawled. It was the same feeling I had when I had tossed the extra wood into the fire and first saw the figure. *Maybe it's an indication of these things*, I thought.

"First-Master Sanjean!" I said in an urgent whisper, my eyes widening as much as they could go and I studied the darkness for any movement aside from our own. "The temperature, did it suddenly get colder for you too?"

He dismissed me with his eyes and pressed forward. "It's the climate, boy, you'll get use to it."

"No, listen!" The urgency in my voice made him stop, as well as the others. "Before I saw the…this thing in the firelight, the air had suddenly gotten a lot colder. The same thing is happening now and I don't think it's a coincidence." There was a pause and I heard Sanjean mumble something incoherently under his breath before he took a step back and look me square in the eyes.

"You say there was a chill, and then afterwards you caught a glimpse of this shadow creature?" He asked.

"Yes, Sir. Odestan felt the cold as well." Which my partner confirmed with a nod of his head.

"As we followed the trail, right before we saw the thing pull out the darkness, it happened again. It only got colder as more of them appeared." I explained. As I spoke tinges of fear wormed their way into my stomach.

"We're going back. Now. What you speak of are Lotarians, and we're not properly equipped to face them." We followed First-Master Sanjean back to the village.

CHAPTER 7: TYLAN
= Lotarians =

After seeing the Lotarians in the woods First-Master Sanjean, Kaleo, Odestan, and myself quickly headed back to the village. The First-Master did not say a word, he only walked hard and swift. Alyn, the First-Masters right hand man, was waiting for us when we returned and asked what we had seen, but Sanjean didn't stop walking. He made a circular motion with his hands to Alyan and the man was off. Despite the hour we went straight to Tomas' house. The rest of the Cabal was waiting for us there. Unceremoniously Sanjean made his way into the house, by knocking down the door, and we followed.

Tomas lived alone and came rushing out of his room at the commotion, a loose shirt and pants hanging around his body. "What is the meaning of this!" Tomas demanded. He was ignored as two men of the Cabal that had followed us in grabbed Tomas by the arms. "Unhand me this instant!" he shouted.

The Masters dragged him into the kitchen and sat him down roughly in one of the chairs. I stood off to the side as the rest of the men filled into the kitchen.

The force of First-Master Sanjean's hand when he slammed it down upon the wooden kitchen table nearly split it in half. The table now sported a large crack that only grew larger when he put his weight down on the table as he leaned forward. "Why didn't you tell us that the Masters that threatened you were working with Lotarians!" He was angry and the words were spat out at Tomas who, to my surprise, held his ground. "We would have been slaughtered before we even knew what was happening!"

"You were told what you needed to know." Tomas said in his defense. "It's not a lie about what happened here."

"The lie was in not telling us the truth about those men and slandering the name of the Schools." First-Master Sanjean pushed off of the table and began heading out of Tomas' house when the old man called him back.

Tomas informed us that the Lotarians had returned. A trader from the Lands Across the Sea spoke of seeing men, and sometimes women, who had soulless eyes and a dark aura that surrounded them. These people brought the coldness of death wherever they went. What he said matched what the stories had said about the Lotarians long ago, only they were not made of shadow. The logical conclusion was that the Lotarians had developed a way to transform people into what were begin called Shadow Men. These creatures were able to walk in the light.

First-Master Sanjean didn't say a word while Tomas spoke, and when his story was done Sanjean left the Elder's house. The rest of us followed after him, leaving Tomas to his own devices.

Though I knew there were things abiding in the Four Kingdoms that could be in any nightmare, I haven't heard of the Lotarians outside of what was in our history books at the School.

As the story goes, the Lotarains were first seen in the Realms five hundred years ago on the outskirts of the Northern Kingdom, in the city of Pomala,. They were discovered by a hunting party who had gone out to find game in the valleys. It was the middle of the night and a few of the men had thought that they had seen something lurking in the woods. The reports said that as they continued to press on into the woods the wind picked up and the night drew chill. From the darkness the shadows came alive and consumed the lead man of the party. More shadows emerged and the others fled. All the men were killed except for one who had managed to make it out of the woods alive and back to the camp where he had told the others of what had happened. As ridiculous as his tale sounded no one believed him at first. When the others were never found, and more people went missing after venturing into the woods at night, his tale looked more and more credible.

Incidents man-eating shadows spread throughout the Realms. The Shaitae, whom would later be known as Ma'Tradoms, said the creatures were known as Lotarians and they shared with the people the creatures weaknesses. Sunlight and fire. The Lotarians spread throughout the land and Shadow War began.

Every household had torches burning outside their doors and windows to keep the Lotarians away. Streets were lined with lanterns and, for a while, everyone carried around a flint and sulfur pouch. For three years the Shaitae's and Masters fought hard alongside the people to drive away the invaders. In the end the Four Kingdoms won the war. The Lotarians were gone but the Realms had suffered gravely. The were cut down to less than half their size and the Masters were nearly eradicated. Dark and dangerous creatures spawned from the earth , their presence a reminder of the shadows that were here. After a few generations had passed without any sign of the Lotarians' return, tales of them and the war were left to the pages of history.

"They had to have been turned into these Shadow Men," I mused to myself. "Why be under the control of the Lotarians? Masters would rather die than be someone's slave." It was a hard concept to wrap my head around. Chulin shrugged next to me, he had been rather placid when we all had gathered back at camp to discuss the details of the night.

"Self preservation." Chulin said with a sagely nod. "It doesn't matter how strong you are. We all have our weaknesses, and we all want to survive. If stuck between a rock and a hard place many people will turn their backs on what they stand for and go to the other side. Besides, would you want your death to be at the hands of a shadow?"

It was fact of human nature, is what he was saying. I couldn't doubt it. I remember this one guy in the school who tired to steal food from one of the Masters tables. He was still hungry after we had been given our meager portions and he wanted more to eat. He knew it was against the rules but he did it anyway. After he was caught his cries echoed throughout the School for hours. I felt no remorse for him. He wasn't starving anymore than the rest of us had been. Some people do things simply out of stupidity.

"Only a fool would turn their back on the School," I said, settling down and trying to get what I could of sleep. The original plan had been to head out at dawn to find the rouge group, but now that First-Master Sanjean knew what we could possibly be up against things had changed. We were going to stay at the village for another day and prepare ourselves to go after the Lotarians and the Shadow Men.

"You're a fool if that's what you think, Tylan," said Samir. "After all the things the Masters have done to us, anyone would want to make them suffer. Masters fighting each other isn't as uncommon as you think."

I cocked a brow as I looked over at him. Unlike the rest of us, Samir wasn't sitting next to the fire thinking of what we were going to do. He was sitting alone. His hook blade laying across his lap and a sanding stone in his other hand. He was busy sharpening his blade. He was always eager to get into some sort of fight so I wasn't surprised. "The Masters beat us. We were starved, deprived of basic needs, even slaves get better treatment than we ever got. It's a wonder that some of them haven't been killed in their beds."

The words made Tao livid and he sprang to his feet. "You shut your mouth you sod!" Before any of us could do anything Tao was on Samir and had thrown the first punch. Samir avoided it with a jovial laugh and slammed Tao in the ribs, knocking him to the ground. Before Tao could get up Samir pulled his sword and pressed its tip against Tao's throat.

"That's enough Samir!" Shouted Kaleo, standing from the fire and looking over at the two. "Stand down!"

"And what if I don't?" Samir said as he pushed the blades tip closer. "I'm not the one who attacked."

Tao laid still on the ground with his hands held out to the side in the manner we were told to do when we were giving on a match. It must have been reactionary. Still, at the same time, his eyes were looking around. I figured that he was trying to find a way to better the other while appearing submitted.

Kaleo approached the two, his hands resting off his side and not near his weapons. "Save your ire for the Lotarians, Samir, not for the Tyro." He was trying to reason with the other man, I could see that, but at the same time I sensed frustration as well.

"There you go again, Kaleo, acting like you know what you're doing when really you are just a coward." At the end of the words Samir had his other blade in hand and it was pointed at Kaleo. It was drawn out so quick that I didn't even seen him reach for it. I had to give it to Samir, he had speed. This was the second time I witnessed those two squaring off, though this was more serious than it had been at the School and I was grateful to not be in the crossfire.

"I've watched you, always hanging by First-Master Sanjean. He's not here to protect you now, is he." Samir was trying to goad Kaleo.

"At least I'm not hiding behind a blade." Kaleo smirked. "This isn't the time for ---"

Kaleo didn't get to finish what he was going to say because Tao, who had been waiting for his opportunity to break free, found it. He made a quick roll to the side - though as the point had been pressing into his skin the move resulted in a surface slice to his neck. Tao got up and reached for his own neck. Kaleo advanced on Samir and knocked the blade out of his hand and forced the guy to the ground. Kaleo's knee pressed against Samir's throat and the tip of his sai was a breath away from Samir's eye.

"Coward! Afraid of a little opposition!" Samir could barely get the words out as his throat was being crushed under the weight of

Kaleo's knee. "You want to beat those around you into submission, just like the Masters."

Kaleo narrowed his eyes. "We respect each other, Samir. If you didn't want to be in the School, then you never should have come."

"You know very well why I'm here," were the cold words that came from Samir. The dark skinned man, even while on the ground as he was, had a foreboding feel. I never noticed it before, perhaps it was only jitters from the days events but there was something about Samir that wasn't right. There was no other way to explain it. No one had moved to help any of the players during the spat, either they knew better - like myself - or they were curious to see what the outcome would be.

"I do know, Samir." Kaleo kept his position a moment longer and then he got up. Putting the sai away he offered Samir a hand up as he stood above him braced and ready to pull when the offer was accepted. Only it wasn't. Samir knocked Kaleo's hand aside and stood under his own power. He picked up his sword and headed to a different spot in our camp.

"Don't you forget the reason you were able to go to the School." Kaleo said to a Samir who was likely no longer listening to anything any of us had to say.

Back turned to the fire Tao was muttering to himself. I looked at Chulin and then at Mikal who was talking in hushed tones to Odestan. There had to be something going on between Samir and Kaleo. While I knew them at the school I had never hung around them enough to learn anything besides the basics of basics. We all had stories to tell of our lives before the School and I would be interested in knowing theirs. For instance, the reason Samir was at the School.

An uneasy silence rested in our camp, even the fires crackle was not as loud. "You all should try to get some rest," Kaleo instructed. "The Lotarians will not be forgiving." Then he moved off to a spot and laid to rest.

I shook my head and sighed.

"He's right you know," Chulin said to me. "Take Samir for example." He was speaking low enough to not easily be overheard. "If he was given the chance, I believe he would turn to the other side."

"Samir's been treated like everyone else at the School." I dismissed the idea. From personal experience I knew that some of the boys were given 'special attention', and not in a good way. The Masters said it was to draw out what they knew we could do. We called that type of attention 'praise'. Anyone could be praised, only some received it more than others. "If he didn't like it there why didn't he leave? We're not prisoners." Or rather, we weren't before we became Tyros. Now we couldn't leave until we reached the Master rank.

"I've always known that Samir wanted to leave the school, he use to talk about it at nights at the end of training," Chulin explained. Unlike myself, he was friends with the guy, and Kaleo too. Those three were together about the same as Odestan and I. "Every time I asked him why didn't he leave he would only say that he couldn't. I wouldn't worry about it. He may not like it, but I don't see him turning his back on us." Chulin ended the conversation by laying on the ground and closing his eyes.

I couldn't rest that easily. I was thinking again. Samir may not betray the Tyro, but that did not mean he wouldn't turn on Kaleo. Groaning inwardly in aggravation I scratched the back of my neck and laid down as well. Back at the School everything had been simple. Out here things only got more and more complicated.

I rested the best that I could that night and during the next day. Nothing out of the ordinary happened and we used the time to get supplies that were needed: mainly heavier clothing for the weather and specially made torches that would burn brighter and longer. I was thankful for the extra clothing - already cold it was only going to be more so when we got around the Lotarains. I had received a long-sleeved black tunic of coarse wool. Having my arms covered felt odd as the only thing that ever covered them before were bracers, but it was a welcome exchange for a bit·of warmth.

First-Master Sanjean and the Cabal were to take the route we followed last night while Kaleo, and the rest of the Tyro were to veer off to the left in hopes of catching the creatures from behind. Our mission was to capture the Shadow Men - kill them if we must. In case we found the Lotarians instead, we were to kill them on sight. A good strategy in theory, I only didn't know if it would work in this case. We weren't dealing with normal people.

Quietly we walked through the damp forest keeping our eyes alert for anything that moved and shadows that were out of place. These woods were full of shadows and it wasn't even fully dark yet. When it started to grow darker we paused and lit the torches. Since

Lotarians were afraid of fire these were probably the best weapons we had.

"I don't like this," I muttered under my breath. We were going to battle creatures we barely knew nothing about outside of outdated history and the hearsay of travelers.

It wasn't long before the night grew bitterly cold. A cry shot through the air - it had come from the direction of the Cabal. The Tyro sprang into action, running to where the sound came from. Our torches lighting the air and filling it with the smell of burning oil and sulfur. Soon we saw the Cabal. If we didn't know what was going on the scene may have even looked comical. Masters were swinging torches and weapons about in the air at shadows. There was no sign of any Shadow Men yet, only the Lotarians.

"Stay sharp!" Warned Kaleo. "They can be anywhere." It was then that I realized I was cold. Being so focused on the night and finding these creatures I had forgotten to pay attention to my own body temperature. "Let's go, and don't let them touch you!"

We ran to help the others.

It was frightening to know that we could run into the backs of these creatures as they blended so well in the darkness. Any shadow could be deadly. From the corner of my eye I saw something move and turned around instantly with my blade in hand and struck out at the night, the torch in my other hand held high. It didn't make contact with anything, but I wasn't fooled. Sword was kept at the ready and I waved the torch around me and looked into the darkness.

I saw nothing, and continued forward. In the hurry to get over to the Cabal and join the rest of my Tyro, I stumbled. The torch flew from my hand and landed in a bush and set it on fire. In the bright light I saw shadow figures heading towards my group. The more of them that I saw the colder I got.

"Coming up on the West side!" I shouted as I got back to my feet. After cautiously plucking the torch from the burning bush I charged at the closest Lotarian. Once I was within distance I swung at him with my blade and . . . nothing!

Nothing. The Lotarian was right there and my sword had gone through him like vapor. I knew that they feared light and fire, but I never knew that they couldn't be hit. They had said nothing about that. The sudden realization made my eyes widen in both shock and fear. If we couldn't hit them.... There wasn't any time to think on it for the creature turned around to attack me. I saw no face, only darkness.

I felt frozen where I stood and in that moment I thought it spoke. "Shaitae," a strange voice crept through the air. "Shaitae!" The Lotarian's arm stretched towards me. Coming to my senses I swung my torch at the creature. It screeched and recoiled backwards from the light, but it didn't leave. The Lotarian stayed at the edge of my firelight.

"TYLAN!" The Lotarian dropped to its knees and burned. Odestan was behind it, his axe blades covered in burning cloth. He had slain the Lotarian and for a moment I was dumbfounded. "Don't just stand there like a ninny! Let's go!"

I followed him into what seemed to be the thick of the battle, leaving the burning Lotarian behind. All around me the men were fighting with their weapons and getting nowhere. The Lotarians were only sliced in half and reformed or turned aside from the fire to come at them from another angle. It was only enough to slow them down. They really were the darkness personified. And darkness was everywhere.

The Cabal had their weapons covered the same as Odestan and were faring better than the Tyro. *Why didn't we know to cover our weapons?* When they were lucky enough to hit, the Lotarian went down. Soon our section of the forest was full of firelight from the fallen, but it was still dark and the night was getting colder and the winds threatened to put out our lights.

"We can't keep this up!" came the shout from First-Master Sanjean. "Retreat back!"

As fast as we could this was accomplished, a line with people standing nearly back to back. We swept the night with our torches while quickly and carefully making our way through the woods. Heaven help us if these creatures ever found a resistance to fire. Nothing moved after us and this made us all a bit jumpy. We didn't trust anything at the moment. Not even our own eyes.

Antone, a member of the Tyro, was walking at my side and I could see the arm that held his sword shaking with nerves. I stepped on a twig and it snapped, Antone jumped and I ducked quickly to avoid the swing of his blade.

"Watch it!" I hissed at him.

"They are out there somewhere. Just waiting for our lights to go out!" His voice was shaking. Then he fell.

"Get up," I urged him. The others who had seen him fall were urging him to do the same. Our line kept moving. We were so conditioned into doing the things that we were told that no one stepped out of formation to help. If he did not get up he would be left behind.

"I can't. I can't get up! My foot is stuck!" Antone sounded frantic. I needed to try and help him. We were moving further away and soon he was outside of our firelight.

"Wait! Man down!" I shouted. "We got to get him up!" I couldn't hear him anymore.

"Help him! quickly!" First-Master Sanjean ordered, and the line paused. A few of us broke line to get him.

When we reached the spot where he fell Antone was nowhere to be seen. We were too late. "Antone! ANTONE!" I yelled. Startled mutterings and soft cries arose from the other men and some of them were even praying to whatever entity would listen. Another piercing scream cut through the air, it sounded like Antone.

"Back to the village, now!" The First-Master ordered. "There's no hope for the lad now and we've got to protect the people."

Odestan was tugging on my arm, his lit axe held high. "Come on! We have to go!"

"We can't just leave him out here!" I said in protest.

"Yes, we can. And we are. We can't help him now."

Odestan was right. In that brief moment Antone had been taken by one of the Lotarians. He was either dead or being turned into a Shadow Man. I didn't know him that well, but he was pat of the Tyro and that made him my brother.

"Come on!" Odestan urged.

I had spent enough time in the dark already - and so had my friend who was risking his own life by lingering out there with me. Without any more thought I ran with Odestan and it wasn't long before we saw the wall of fire that made up the outer part of the village.

We stopped inside the fire wall. Catching our breaths while we looked out into the night for any signs of the Lotarians. The remaining Tyros looked unnerved, and were covering their weapons in cloth like the Cabal had. When I looked at the Cabal members they were in a huddle and were speaking in low tones.

Kaleo approached and punched me on the shoulder. His eyes were wild and his breathing was heavy from the fear that all of us had experienced and from the cold we were not use to. "What happened back there? You let Antone fall. We lost one of our men because of you!"

"What?" I didn't appreciate how Kaleo was speaking to me, or the fact that he was so quick to blame me for what had happened to our comrade when I was the only one who tried to help.

"Antone has paid the price for your incompetence!" Kaleo swung at me and caught his fist. I was mad after Antone was taken, but now I was furious.

"I stepped on a twig!" I shouted back at Kaleo. "He jumped at the sound and fell! How is that my fault!"

"You should have caught him!" Kaleo hit me in the side with his other fist and I let go of his hand to defend myself. Suddenly Odestan was pulling me off my feet and away from Kaleo. Both Mikal and Tao had tackled him and were holding him to the ground.

"He's gone!" Kaleo yelled. "He's gone!"

By this time townsfolk had come close to the firewall and were watching us from a distance.

"Stop it, both of you!" Came the booming voice of First-Master Sanjean. He had broken away from his group and was now standing between the two of us. "If you're going to act like children I'll toss you both into the woods myself and let you fend off the Lotarians! We'll see if you last the night with no fire!"

There was a sternness to Sanjean's face but there also was disappointment in the back of his eyes. But, when he looked at me I saw annoyance.

Odestan let me go and I stepped away, shrugging my shoulders and shaking out my hands. My friend stayed near, just in case I decided to throw a punch at Kaleo who was also being allowed to get to his feet. I wouldn't attack Kaleo with the First-Master standing right there, but I was still angry and I had questions I wanted answered.

I wiped my mouth with the back of my hand and then spat at the ground. "First-Master Sanjean." I called out to him and immediately knew that I would regret the next thing I was about to say, but I said it anyway. In public, where everyone could hear me.

"You knew the Lotarians couldn't be destroyed with our weapons. Didn't you." I dared to look him in the eyes as I made my accusation. I saw his expression change, but he didn't reply so I continued on. "You knew. What you said yesterday, while we were with Tomas, that we would be slaughtered. You knew that our weapons wouldn't be of any use against the Lotarians but you said nothing."

This caused a bit of a stir in the Tyros and the Cabal. First-Master Sanjean stepped close to me. A heaviness in his step he squared out his shoulders and tipped his head back to look down at me. The man was very broad of shoulder and towering over me as he was there was an imposing force about him. I held my ground. I had started this fight, I had to see it through.

"What exactly are you saying, boy." The way he said 'boy' was as cold as a Lotarian air.

"You sent us out there to die. That's what I'm saying. Sir." I don't know what gave me the nerve to say those words to him, to make such a claim without any proof, or what compelled me to keep going. I was angry about Antone. I was confused about why the Lotarian had stood there instead of attacking me. Behind me Odestan whispered harshly that I should shut up.

"Why did every member of the Cabal know to wrap their weapons in cloth and set them on fire? You couldn't have told us that before we left and given us a fighting cha—"

His hit was one that I couldn't avoid. It was quick, it was heavy, and I swore that my skull cracked open as I flew back and hit the ground. My head hurt so bad that I couldn't begin to get up. It took everything I had to try and breathe after having the wind knocked out of me from the fall. First-Master Sanjean's foot then pressed down on my chest.

"Now listen to me you worthless sod," First-Master Sanjean's voice leaked of anger, and it was all directed at me. The realization that he would kill me at that moment if it wasn't for the Code holding him back came to life. He pressed down harder on my chest and I cried out in pain. The cracked rib that I sustained back at the School the morning we left was undoubtedly broken once more along with cracks in a few others. "I look out for my men and I take responsibility for the things that befall them. If you ever, ever think of slandering my name and actions like that again I will cut out your tongue and make you wear it around your own neck."

His threat was clear even if my charges to him had gone unanswered. My words were said and maybe others of the Tyro would question what had happened tonight.

It was getting increasingly harder to breath. My hands grabbed at his foot and I tried to push him off. He only pressed down harder, causing me to cough and wheeze. I needed air.

"Do you understand me, Tyro!" He shouted down at me. "Answer me!"

My reply came in the nodding of my head and then with a strained 'yes'. Only then did he pull his foot off my chest and I rolled to my right side, curling in on myself like a ball and taking in as much air as I could. Every breath was pain. I wrapped my arms around my chest and felt hands helping me to a sitting position. I vaguely heard First-Master Sanjean call out for a physician and remark that we were leaving at first light. Then, I passed out.

CHAPTER 8 : SCOTIA
= The Impossible Stranger =

It was the smell of sulfur that woke me up. I have never been a fan of the way the oder coated my throat and picked at my nose. I did not know what was worse: the burning smell of sulfur or the banging pressure in my head.

There was a rumble and a jolt, the sound of metal irons clanging against each other and I slid across a coarse floor. That's when I opened my eyes and almost immediately shut them again. The pain in my head nearly doubled and I tried to bring my hands to my head but they were heavily ladened down. "What? What's going on here? Maerilea? Maerilea!" I called out frantically.

"Quiet in there, or I'll gag you!" Came the shout of a rough voice I didn't recognize.

I slowly opened my eyes and saw that I was in a wooden wagon with black metal bars. It was the type used by slavers. My hands and legs were clapped in heavy irons and tethered together with a chain. Feeling trapped brought about a sense of fear and panic that only grew when I saw I was alone. Where was Maerilea? The last thing I could remember was holding her tightly around the stomach and begging for her to help me as the Master converged upon us.

Phyllis. That woman wasn't nice at all and the Master was nothing like the teachings said. He was wanting to take us, is that what happened and why I was chained inside of this wagon? Where was my friend?

It was night outside and without a lot of light I couldn't see where I was going. I crawled over to the bars and began to shake and pull at them, vainly hoping that they would give and I wasn't surprised when they didn't budge. Looking around my small space I couldn't see a door. Surrounded on three sides by bars the only solid surfaces were the floor, ceiling and the front that separated me from the owner of the voice.

"There's no use in trying to escape from there," said the voice from beyond the wall. "The bars are solid and so are your chains. Do not worry, we'll be there shortly."

"Where am I!" I cried, throwing myself against the solid wall before recoiling from the pain to my shoulder and the loudness of the chains. I could still smell the burning sulfur but didn't know where it was coming from. Perhaps it came from a light the driver was using. I tossed my head to push my hair out of my vision and then huddled against that wall. "What do you want with me!"

It was cold and I shivered. My dress was gone. The only thing I wore was my cotton shift, leggings and shoes. Abandoned - again- and the thought of it hurt. If mother had never taken me from the Order this would never have happened. I didn't know what had become of her after the fire in the tavern in Ravensbro, and now I didn't even have Maerilea. Things kept getting worse and I didn't know what to do. I could try to use my Kenisis to stop the wagon, but then what? There was nothing I could do about these chains and I would be caught again. I drew my knees to my chest and hung my head down and began to cry.

"That's more like it," said the voice. He had heard my tears. "Cry. You're already broken."

He started to laugh. I heard it. He was laughing at me. Laughing at how weak I was. "You think that's funny!" I yelled, scrubbing my eyes with the back of my hand. "You think you're so powerful! Capturing a small girl like me; calling yourself powerful!"

'So much locked away potential.' I remembered Aquali saying that about me to others when she thought that I couldn't hear her. Potential. I didn't know why she would say that, especially considering how much of a failure I was in her classes, but I was going to show this man how broken I really was! I could either sit in this wagon and accept what was going to happen, or I could fight. I was going to fight.

It was dark out so I couldn't rely on my vision but this was a road, and a road was made up of earth. *Just one time*, I prayed, *let this work*. I closed my eyes and fixed a mental picture of a road, slightly straight and rocky. Now all I had to do was focus. Know what I wanted to do, feel it happening, and have faith that it was. Using the Kenisis took a lot of faith. It was known that the strength of the wielder's belief in what they were doing determined the strength of the doing. Right now faith in myself was in low supply. I had depended on other people so much that I was unsure on how to do it on my own.

The wagon shook again, this time more violently than it had the first time and I heard the driver call out to settle the horse. I ignored it the best I could. In my head I pictured a hole in the road big enough for the wagon wheel to get stuck. The depth of it and the length able to capture both front wheels; and wide enough that it wasn't easily travelled over. The hole was there. It had to be there, just a bit more up the road. I wrapped my arms tightly around my legs and held on to that thought as hard as I could. It seemed to take forever, but then the wagon lurched forward and I heard a crack! The horse brayed at the jolt and I fell to the side. It worked! The wagon was stuck!

The driver cracked his whip, urging the horse to move, to pull harder. I got to my hands and knees and crawled over to the bars and looked at the ground. With the aid of the flickering lamp light I saw shards of broken wood laying about and assumed the wagon wheel had broken. What luck! Not only had I successfully stopped the wagon, but the wheel was broken as well! Now I only had to figure out a way of escape.

The wagon rocked as the driver jumped down from his seat. He was board of shoulder with a clean shaved head. Tanned skin with a scar that ran down the left side of his face, he also wore a Masters symbol on his belt. Likely this was the other man who had arrived at Phyllis' home. He saw me looking out the bars and cracked his whip against them. "Think you're so smart! I'm going to take payment for that wheel out of your flesh. C'mere, girly!"

He pushed up on one of the bars and it went up along with the ones next to it. There must have been a latch there I couldn't see in the dark. I screamed. My screaming would either call people to his aide or to mine, but it was worth a shot. I inched across the floor, trying to put as much distance between him and myself as I could in that small wagon. The driver put down the whip and jumped into the wagon. Grabbing my chains he pulled me towards him. He laughed as I kicked and continued to scream. "Quiet!" He yelled and then he struck me on the face.

There was a noise at the front and the wagon shook. The driver let go if my chains and grabbed the blade at his side. "Don't move," he warned and stepped out of the cage to see what was going on. My face was sore but I couldn't focus on that now. I didn't know what was going on, but as soon as the opening was clear, I was going to try to escape.

A man suddenly jumped from the front of the wagon and tackled the driver to the ground. In that moment the door was clear. The two men were fighting against the wagon. Who was this guy to take on a Master? "RUN!" The stranger shouted to me before he met the oncoming attack of my captor.

Taking the opportunity I fell out the wagon and landed hard on the ground. It was a struggle but I got to my feet and ran as much as the chains would allow. When I fell I inched my way along the ground. One way or another I was going to get away and hide myself. I caught glimpses of the fight and saw the other man barely thwarting the attacks of the Master. He was doing his best to keep the Master from coming after me. Another time I would have liked to watch the match as I had never seen one, but now was not that time.

I focused on my escape and tried to connect to the Kenisis, willing the grass to come up and hide me, or the earth to sink in and take me away. Anything. My mind was a frantic mess of chaos and panic and the only thought I had was escape. My heart was in my throat and my body ached with exhaustion and pain but madly I continued. From the direction of the wagon I heard a grunt, then I thought I heard sounds of people approaching. The Master had said that we were almost there, what if the sounds came from the people who were waiting for us? They were not going to get me!

Fast steps were approaching me from behind me and I tried to go faster. I dare not to call out incase the person couldn't see me - even of the clink-clank of the chains sounded off like a beacon. Soon hands roughly pulled at my waist and I was yanked from the ground like a sack. Being now held against the persons chest, a rough, and dirty, hand closed over my mouth. I kicked and failed about trying to free myself. The more I struggled the tighter the hold around my waist got.

"Calm down or I'll let them find you!" Came a harsh whisper to my ear. "Trust me and I'll get us out of here."

This couldn't have been the Master who had me in the wagon, he wouldn't have been so kind. I assumed it was the stranger. I didn't have to trust him, but right now I didn't really have much of a choice. I stopped struggling but kept my guard up.

"That's better. Stay really still." He instructed and he pushed his back up against a tree. It was unnerving to have my feet off the ground but I accepted it. His dirty hand put a bad taste in my mouth that I tried to ignore. There were more important things to be troubled over.

In our current silence I heard sounds in the forest around me of people looking for us and smelled fire from their torches. "We're going to have to make a run for it," the man whispered.

Then, without any warning, he shot out from the tree, tossing me over his shoulder as he ran. His hold was so tight that it hurt.

Someone shouted, "There they are!" and my current captor cursed.

"Here they come!" I shouted the obvious. "Go faster!" Thinner than the other guys who were after us he seemed to have an advantage when it came to getting over hurdles and he practically flew through the forest, even carrying me in the heavy chains. Soon the lights from the other guys began to fall far behind and they were only spots against the darkness. There was direction to this mans running and he turned into a thick of trees where a horse was waiting. Unceremoniously he flung me on the saddle and hoped on behind me.

"Here we go!" He shouted as he kicked the horse into motion. We were off, riding hard down the road and into the darkness.

He pressed the horse hard. It made the ride terribly uncomfortable for me, especially since he had thrown me across the horses neck and any adjustment I wanted to make had me afraid that I would fall off. He could have sat me up at least! We rode for the remainder of the night and left the main road once the sun came up. The sun was in front of us, we were heading east. I had not heard anyone behind us for a long while and thought that we had lost the Master and that group. Once the terrain had gotten to dense to keep up the fast pace, the man stopped the horse and dismounted.

"We walk from here," he said, pulling the reigns over the horses head and walked forward, guiding the horse as he went. "Or rather, I walk. Can't have you falling and breaking a leg."

With the length of my chains and the properties of the forest floor, I had to agree. I was more likely to fall and get tangled than make any progress. I still didn't know whether this man was a help, or if I had traded one capture for another. I hadn't seen any Master markings on him, but that didn't mean he couldn't have taken it off.

There was another problem. "Could you at least, please, sit me up?" Still laying across the saddle, now that he was gone I felt less secure and didn't dare move. "I feel very faint."

"If you were going to faint you would have done so by now and we wouldn't be having this conversation." He didn't even bother to look at me when he spoke.

"Just because I haven't fainted yet, doesn't mean that I won't!" I tried to appeal to him but he wasn't listening. I huffed in aggravation and tried to worm my way further up on the horse. So far my experience with males was not a positive one. Not in the least. Thankfully my shift that I wore was long - if not very dirty - but I could have done with another layer of clothing. Without him riding in the seat I was exposed again to the cold.

I managed to hook my elbow around the horn of the saddle and mustered what strength I could and pulled with my arms while trying to lift both legs at once. The horse made a small jump and I yelped as I nearly fell off, the only thing that saved me was the hold on the saddle horn. The horse stopped and I saw the man grinning at me. It was then that I decide that I didn't like him. My supposed rescuer. He could have helped me instead of staring there watching. I suppose he thought he was helping enough by having stopped the horse.

With a few grunts and extra strain I was able to pull my legs up. I was now laying flat on the horse instead of tossed like a sack and it felt much better. He was still watching me, impatiently, and I pulled myself up to sitting side saddle. I fleet sore in every part of my body but I looked at him defiantly. He rolled his eyes at me and got the horse moving again.

"You know, I don't even know who you are." I said, vastly proud of myself for not needing any help to sit up on the horse. "For all I know I could have been better off with the other guy and his men." Which I knew wasn't true. Perhaps if I was better at using the Kenisis I would have been okay but right now, what I had done with the wagon was more luck than skill. The same applied to now: I was to mentally and physically tired to try anything.

"If you really feel that way then I'll drop you off here and leave the men to get you. I doubt you will be hard to find, or catch, with your chains attached." He said. For a brief moment I thought that he was kidding but then he stopped the horse. I heard him sigh and then he turned and approached.

"Look. You can either be quiet and let me do the job I was hired to do, or I can let you go here and I'll report back that you're dead. That's what you will be without me. Dead." His explanation to me was straight and plain. There was no hint of playfulness in his voice, or that he wouldn't do what he said. It didn't stop me from having questions.

"Who hired you?" That part had me the most curious, next to that was why those other men would kill me. Sell me, keep me as a slave, sure, but kill me?

His eyes were fixed on me for what had to have only been a couple of seconds, but his dark brown gaze held such intensity and strength in them that I momentarily forgot to breathe. Even the wagon driver, when I saw his face, didn't have eyes like this man here. It made me wonder about his story.

"Governor Rycliff," he said. My eyes widened. "And your mother."

The last thing he said had me in such a state of shock that I nearly fell off the horse. "My...my mother?" This meant that she was still alive! That put me a bit at ease, though why wasn't she out looking for me instead of sending someone else?

"You seem surprised," was his comment and he pulled the horse into motion once again, this time holding on to the bridal and staying next to me. "You were suppose to go to Certima; and if you had done as you were told I wouldn't have had to come all the way out here to fetch you."

Now he was scolding me? "Were you sent to find Maerilea too? We were both suppose to go to Certima together." I was hopeful that he had already found her, or that he was going to do so. I didn't know what happened to her and after what had happened last night I was very concerned of her fate.

"I am to bring you to the Governor, not go out of my way to find her." He said, his words straight and clear. "She's only my responsibility if she happened to be with you. Since she isn't, it's no concern of mine."

"No concern!" I scoffed in disbelief and panic. I noticed the terrain was becoming rockier, we were heading towards the mountains, which meant that he wasn't going to cross the chasm. We couldn't have passed over it already or else now we would be going backwards from our destination.

"She's my friend! My best friend! She's only in this mess because of me and I can't just leave her out here to whatever is out there!" I stated. If there were people after me, maybe the same people were after her. Or already had her! Oh Maerilea!

"Then you should have kept an eye on her." Came his response and he motioned forward. "We'll stay there for a while so you can rest."

'There' happened to be an old abandoned cabin. The sides of it were covered with vines and moss, one side of the place was torn down. From how it looked on the outside I could only imagine what it was like internally. He teetered the horse to a tree close to the cabin and came to get me off of the horse. Instead of putting me on the ground so that I could walk, he tossed me over his shoulders. Pulling the travel sack off the horse he flung it over his other shoulder.

"I'm not a sack of potatoes you know." I said in protest, but he didn't respond, only continued walking. I huffed in aggravation.

The door to the cabin wasn't locked so it opened with a push. I could only imagine what the house was like in its prime. Inside there were remnants of furniture, most of it was broken. The fireplace looked usable and the bed had been taken off its feet and simply sat on the ground. That is where he sat me down. It was made out of straw, but compared to my last two surfaces, it felt delightful. Now that I was sitting more comfortably than I had been for hours my body began to give in to its fatigue. I pulled my knees to my chest and watched as the man poked the fireplace with a stick and pulled out some debris.

"You never told me your name." I said quietly.

I was about to say it again - because he gave no response - when he spoke. "It's Benjamin. I have to get wood for a fire." He stood and tossed the travel sack next to me. "There's water and a bit of food in the pocket. I suggest you eat."

Just like that he left out the door and was gone. I watched for a moment, thinking that he was going to come back through the door and moment, but it stayed closed and my eyes were getting heavy. As my throat was parched I pulled the flask of water from the sack and took a long drink. It felt good to finally wet my throat. I wished he had clothes in the sack, or at least a blanket. A fire would be wonderful.

Yawning I sat the flask down and rested my head upon my knees and sighed. I knew more than I had last night, but I also had more questions. My mother was alive and had sent this man, Benjamin, out to find me. How did she escape and why was I being hunted by Masters? It all had to do with Certima, I was certain of it now. How long was I going to stay in these chains?

My eyes were feeling heavier by the moment, I even tried shaking my head to wake up more as I wanted to wait until Benjamin came back and ask him my questions. That wasn't going to happen for my eyes shut and I was sleep.

I woke up hours later to the sound of a crackling fire and I sighed in joy as I wasn't cold anymore. I actually smiled. I must have been asleep for a while as the light that came in from the broken roof had the color of sunset. Everything here was quiet and still. I noticed Benjamin resting against the wall by the bed. His eyes were closed and I leaned closer to him to see if he was actually asleep. Benjamin was older than me, maybe in his early twenties, and he wore a black tunic etched in a dull silver. The colors looked familiar, though I saw no crest or symbol to mark him as anything more than a commoner in well made clothes. Physically he didn't look much different than the people I had seen back at the tavern, yet he had fought against a Master and was able to walk away.

"It's about time you woke up," he said through partially parted lips. Startled, I blinked and sat back. Now that he was awake Benjamin moved over to the fire and retrieved what looked like pliers. "I had thought of doing this while you were still asleep since I wanted to leave here before the afternoon, but decided to let you sleep...." Benjamin drew that out while looking at me like I had spoiled his plans. I suppose that I had in a way.

"Sorry...." That was all I could think of to say and I looked curiously at the pliers. "What are those for?"

Without a word he reached out and pulled my chains forward. "Hey! You don't have to be so rough."

"Stay still."

He did just what I thought he was going to do - put the pliers against the chains and cut. I heard the snap and could have rejoiced! Finally I was able to move my legs and arms freely again, but the bracelets were still there. they were so close to the skin, wide and thick that the pliers wouldn't fit without cutting me as well. He put the pliers down.

"Wait. W-what about the bracelets?" I questioned, holding my hands out to him. "The bracelets are a bit thick but you could try." It was worth the risk.

"Be patient," he said and motioned for me to give him one of my legs. I gave him my left one, but he didn't pick the pliers back up. Instead he wrapped his hands around the bracelet and gave me a warning. "Be still."

What was he going to do? The bracelet was too tight for it to slip off so he couldn't have been thinking of pulling it off. As he held my leg I felt the metal warm though it did not burn. Then I heard a crack and Benjamin pulled his hand away from my leg, the metal bracelet broken in half his hands. My eyes widened in disbelief and my mouth fell open. I stared at him, unblinking, as he took my other leg and repeated whatever it was he had done.

I swallowed hard and shook my head. "That's...not possible." There was no record of a man wielding any type of power, though that is exactly what Benjamin had done. "This simply isn't possible! What are you!"

CHAPTER 9: SCOTIA
= Friends and Enemies =

Benjamin looked at me and rolled his eyes before he reached for one of my hands. "I'm a man. I thought that much was obvious to you."

His attitude about the matter wasn't appreciated, but it paled in comparison to what he was able to do to free me. I stayed perfectly still, perhaps I was afraid to move because I didn't know what was going to happen if I moved. I wasn't afraid of magical abilities - I had them myself - but he was a male.

"But, you're not suppose to be able to do that." I said, finally finding my voice as the bracelet dropped off of my right arm. Benjamin put his hands around the last bracelet. I leaned forward to get a closer look at his face. Maybe I could see something there, but I couldn't see anything. I wasn't even sure what I was trying to see.

"There are no records of this. At all. How are you able doing this?" I was slightly jealous. He was a male. He was not even suppose to be able to do anything like this and it seemed as natural as breathing. It took all the concentrated effort I had to even make the hole in the road that stopped the wagon! And, he was manipulating meal. "I can't even do that."

Bending metal, that's what he was doing, right? Being able to work metals wasn't one of the Kenisis either. There were five Kinesis: Geo, Aero, Pyro, Hydro, and Lumo, though the last hasn't been seen in anyone for hundred of years. What he was doing could be part of the GeoKenisis, but no Ma'Tradom on record had been able to do what he was either! This brought about the question, again, of who he was and if my mother knew of his ability.

Once the bracelets were gone, I rubbed my wrist. It felt good to be free again. Benjamin moved away from me, taking the metal remains and tossing them in the fire. "That's not anything I know. I haven't read anything like what you just did. Who else knows about this?"

"There are a lot of things you don't know, Scotia. Some things are better that way." He went to the door and looked out. "If you always go about expecting things to be one way, you're setting yourself up to be fooled." This was his advice to me, though truthfully I didn't fully understand what he meant.

I got up and followed Benjamin, finding myself mystified in this new found revelation about him. "How are you able to hold power?" I asked him softly, maybe he would answer.

"It's been that way since I was a boy. It's not a big deal."

I barely held in a puff of laughter. "Not a big deal? It's a huge deal! It's...it's groundbreaking that's what it is!" I exclaimed. "You may be the only male out there able to do what you do. Can you do other things?"

"I'm not a side show entertainment!" He snapped and glared at me. I must have hit a nerve.

I looked at him with wide eyes, trying to keep my fear in check. The look in his eyes was hard and violent. Though it faded quickly, I had seen it. How did he get eyes like those. I stumbled on the words I tried to say, "I was only ---"

"It doesn't matter," Benjamin interrupted me and motioned towards the fire. "Put out the fire and come on. We need to get moving."

##

When we left the run down cottage he didn't walk the horse like I thought, instead he set out at a run once more and that only made me cold again. I still only wore the shift and it wasn't that thick. The horse covered some of the air, and my back was fully covered by Benjamin - who let me ride proper this time - but the shift ran up my thighs and my arms were nearly bare.

Benjamin kept the horse off of the main roads, sticking mostly to the trees and footpaths. We were heading north and the thick forest was steadily being replaced by mountains. It would take longer getting to Certima this way then taking the valley that separated the Southern Kingdom from the East, and crossing over the chasm bridge, but he had said people were expecting us to take the valley and this was safer. Sometimes we would go miles and miles before we saw another another person as not many lived in the mountains. The weather was harsh and large beast were said to roam the higher regions.

When we did pass people some of them would give us an odd look, almost like it was surprising to see two people riding together. Some even bowed their heads as we went by. Benjamin either ignored it, or didn't see it. Maybe they looked because I was mess and underdressed for the mountainous air. The last time I had a chance to bathe was the morning that Phyllis had betrayed Maerilea and I. Since then I've been in the dirt, stripped of my clothing, bounced around on a horse, and slept on a hay bed. I bet I looked the part of a beggar. At least Benjamin looked groomed. Feeling self conscious I brought up my hands to finger comb through my hair.

"The reward must be pretty good for you to search all over the Four Kingdoms to find me." I mentioned casually. "Governor Rycliff can have just about anyone he wants."

"If you would rather take your chances on traveling to Certima alone, I'll let you off and be on my way." Was his response. I couldn't tell if he was kidding or not but the other day he was ready to drop me off while I was still in chains. I doubted the feeling changed.

The more he avoided my questions spurred on my need to know. It didn't make sense to me as to why someone would go through all the trouble for me. I wasn't a Ma'Tradom, I wasn't very skilled in the Kenisis at all. I had only seen my mother two other times in my life before this adventure began. I couldn't believe that she cared so much as to hire a bounty hunter to find me.

After a while of riding I started to feel ill, that's the only way I could describe it. Maybe it was the monotony of travel or the stress of everything that had happened. My head hurt and my stomach pulled in on itself. I was only hungry. I couldn't remember the last time I actually ate something. My stomach growled and I curled over my arms that I wrapped around myself to dampen the sound. Benjamin heard it and then he sighed. "I know where we can stop for food and you can clean yourself up." He said. "It won't be much longer."

I felt like such a bother to him. "Are you hungry?" I asked, turning to look at him.

"You shouldn't ask to many questions," was the only thing he said and I groaned in frustration.

"Can't you give me a straight answer for once!"

"Possibly."

Benjamin was completely infuriating.

It was about midday when we arrived at a small mountain village, and even though the sun was sitting high in the sky it was still cold. The town was less than half the size of Ravensbro.

"I don't think I like this town." I said to myself, even if he was there to hear it. Unlike the bustling city this one had a slow pace about it. I wondered if they were miners since they were in the mountains. There were people meandering about their business or talking to each other in the streets. A few kids here and there, but many people we saw were going about daily task and chores. I didn't see what looked like an Inn anywhere.

Benjamin seemed to know where he was going for the horse never stopped long enough for him to consider a destination. A few people tipped their hats to him and he gave a nod in return. *Oh, so he's been here before. Maybe he came through here on his way to find me?*

The horse stopped at a humble house that already had a horse hitched out front. There was an older man sitting in a chair on porch and smoking a pipe. A woman - his wife perhaps - was beating a line of clothes off to the side of the house, but she turned her attention to us as we neared. From the looks of it they were rather simple folk and it got a smile out of me, even if it was more out of embarrassment.

Benjamin got off the horse and tethered it next to the other one without saying anything to the old man who was watching him. The lady came from the side of the house, a basket of clothes under her left arm. "What did you bring for us this time?" Unlike Phyllis' voice this woman's had kindness and her smile had nothing to hide. A curious expression upon her face as she looked me over, her free hand straightening the apron she wore over her heavy skirt "Did you bring a girl with you, Benjamin?" I lowered my head under the weight of her eyes and she chortled. "It's hard to tell under all the grit and grime."

Hearing that I squared my shoulders and pushed back my hair. There wasn't anything I could do about my appearance, especially since I was still sitting on the horse for all to see.

"Judy...." Benjamin said, slightly reprimanding her with a smile. He never smiled at me like that, even if he was scolding the lady, it was a smile I never got. "Be nice. She's had a hard ride." To my surprise he put his hands around my waist and lifted me off of the horse. He set me on the ground in front of Judy.

"Hi..." I said nervously, wishing that I could hide myself. I didn't even have shoes to cover my feet. Judy didn't speak to me, only started ushering me away with one arm around my shoulders and removing me from Benjamin, taking me up the steps of the home. I may not have liked Benjamin but he was the only person

94

here I knew. After what happened the last time I was in a strangers home I didn't want to be separated from the only person I knew. Benjamin returned the horse. I opened my mouth to ask what was going on but he only nodded his head for me to go with Judy, and so I did and attempted to mask my fears.

"Riding with you, I'm surprised she's still in one piece." Judy remarked over her shoulder. Then she addressed me, "Come on, child. Let's get you washed up and presentable." She opened the front door and I went through. The old man hadn't said a word the entire time.

Benjamin watched the ladies until the front door closed behind them. He sighed and scrubbed his hand over his head. He kept his tightly curled black hair so short it was a wonder why he simply didn't go bald. A few strokes were given to the horses' mane before Benjamin pulled the saddle bag off the horses back and tossed it over his shoulder. Shadow Men had tracked him here the last time he passed through this village. They had caused a lot of damage and the people blamed him for it. Judy had been the only one to believe he wasn't at fault.

"I didn't think we'd see you back here so soon," the old man on the porch spoke up.

Benjamin had been heading up the steps and to the door, but now he stopped. "Sorry to disappoint." Really he wasn't.

The old man stood up and partially blocked the front door. Benjamin made no move to push past him, instead he waited, his right hand holding tightly to the saddle bag handle.

"Don't think that you can walk into this town, into my home, after everything that happened the last time you were here, and receive a warm welcome." The man's warning was given in low tones so that it wouldn't reach the people inside. "If it were not for that young girl, you wouldn't have been given a second glance."

"Good thing I have the girl then, huh?" Benjamin even cocked a grin at the man, but he didn't do anything else.

"You are not welcome here," the old man stated.

"Thanks for the tip," Benjamin said before he walked past the old man and into the house.

##

It felt really good to be doing something as basic as taking a bath. Judy had opened up their washroom to me and filled the coated wooden tub with hot water and also provided soap, a towel, and a change of clothes. I was curious as to how this tub held the water being that it was made out of wood. I thought that the water would seep out, but it didn't. Back at the Order the tubs were glass - I always said it was so that the Ma'Tradoms could tell how well the Novilites had cleaned them. Needless to say, there wasn't much for modesty back at the Order for certain things either. Maybe that's because we were all women. Since I've left there I've become increasingly aware of my own body and the looks I received from both male and female.

I had never considered myself to be beautiful like some of the other girls in the Order. I wasn't particularly tall with the the full figure and silky hair, my hair was thick and with a heavy curl. My skin tone was a few shades lighter than Benjamin's. There were other girls there who looked like me as far as skin tone was concerned, but they were always so regal and delicate, even in the way they worked the Kenisis. I scooted down deeper in the water until it was at my chin and I drew my knees up to my chest. It was a comforting position even if the water was now only room temperature. Guess I had been in the washroom a while.

I started to think about my friend, Maerilea. Where was she now and was she okay? Sighing inwardly I drew in a deep breath, held it, and sunk down under the water.

The door to the washroom opened up and Benjamin came inside.

I was shocked. At first I had thought that it was Judy come to tell me that my time was up, come eat, or something else. Lifting my head and shoulders out of the water, I wiped a hand down my face and saw Benjamin was in the room. "What are you doing here?" I asked. The room wasn't exactly large and he was standing pretty close to the tub. I covered myself with legs and arms, glad that the water still had me covered. "Get out!"

"I need to talk to you." He replied

"Now?" I sunk more into the water. I had been trying to have a decent conversation with this man for the past couple of days and he wanted to talk now? My face was burning; no doubt my cheeks were red of embarrassment. This guy pulled feeling out of me that I didn't know how to describe. "Could it not wait until after I --- oh!"

Benjamin threw the towel at me while I was talking and it half landed in the water. "Dry off and dress while I talk. We need to leave."

I looked at him now with disbelief. "Leave? What do you mean leave?" We had only just gotten here and I had thought that we were going to stay for the night and get a decent meal - I still hadn't eaten as Judy said I couldn't have anything until I was clean.

"Either you get out, or I pull you out." I was learning that Benjamin expected obedience. He wasn't making an idle threat.

"Okay, okay." I narrowed my eyes at him while I held the towel to the tub. If he wanted me to get out then he would have to at least have the decency to turn around. After a moment he rolled his eyes and turned to face the door.

"This town is under the watch of Lotarians and —"

"The Lotarians haven't been around for hundreds of years," it was my turn to do the interrupting, though he didn't seem to take kindly to it as his head turned and he set hardened eyes at me. I was in the middle of climbing out the tub, one foot poised in the air. With his look I jumped out and scrambled to wrap the wet towel around. Before I could say anything more he turned his head back around and continued his story.

"And they know you're here. We need to leave before the sun sets to give us a fighting chance. I may be be able to hold some of them off, but not all of them. Their Shadow Men followed me last time and I thought I saw one or two of them on our arrival. We need to go before they realize they were seen." He picked up the pile of clothes that Judy had set out for me to wear and offered them over his shoulder.

Hanging the towel off the side of the tub I took the clothes and began to dress. "I don't understand. What are Shadow Men? Why are coming for me?" It didn't make any sense to me at all.

"You don't know do you?" He asked. "You honestly don't know. I thought you were playing dumb."

"Know what?" I couldn't help my curiosity. My fingers slowed on tying the strings to my leather bodice. It felt good to be clean and decently clothed again.

Benjamin turned back around. I didn't mind as I was nearly dressed. The look in his eyes was appraising and I was suddenly very cautious of how I looked. *Why does he keep looking at me like that?* What she had given me to wear had a familiarity about it as I wore something similar in the Order. A thick shift underneath a tunic gown of brown, though over that was a leather bodice of darker color and it tied up the front. This was the common dress of a working girl in the Eastern Kingdom.

"You're mother, Scotia, is a Shaitae. A pure Shaitae, not a small percentage like the Ma'Tradoms today. She comes from one of the Lands Beyond the Sea." Benjamin explained.

I couldn't believe what he had just said. "You're lying. She can't be." I accused him. My head spinning. The Shaitae did a lot of good, but also a lot of evil. Many say the Lotarians came to the Realms because of them and that the Shadow War was their fault, brought on by the Shaitae's greed for power. After the Shadow War they formed the Order and became the first Ma'Tradoms. Everyone in the Order was of Shaitae decent. "More Shaitaes never came to the Realms," I said. "Not even years later. There are no records of it in the histories." There was no record of men with abilities either, but Benjamin was living proof.

Benjamin said, "I don't know what stories your Order has spun to you about the Ma'Tradoms, but I'd bet most of it are lies. Believe what I tell you. There are more Shaitae just as there are Lotarians and their Shadow Men - people like those Masters who captured you,. They work for the Lotarians. They're looking for you. We have to leave."

What he had said was a lot for me to take in at one time. I felt overwhelmed and my head was spinning. The Shaitaes could use the Kenisis naturally. If I was in the direct line then what was wrong with me? "What's so important about me?" That was a question I really wished he would answer. "What about my brother? They'll be after him the same."

Benjamin said nothing for a moment and was soft when he spoke. "As long as there are Shaitae the Lotarians cannot take over the Realms. War is already beginning. The Shaitae are few. The Lotarians are many. Innocent people will continue to die unless we defeat them."

I was surprised at his answer and did not know how to respond. Benjamin looked away from me then and I breathed a bit easier. I hadn't seen my brother since I was left at the Order all those years ago and Benjamin said nothing about his state. I barely remembered him. We probably wouldn't recognize the other.

Benjamin opened the door and I reached out and grabbed his arm. "Benjamin?" There was no 'yes' from him but he had turned to look at me. I took that to mean that I could ask. "What's so important about Certima?" A lot of what I had been told still did not make any sense, but we were still going to Certima, and my brother supposedly as well. "If the Lotarians are after us, wouldn't it be safer to go to the Order? They did defeat them last time."

"Remember what I said - the Lotarian's have Shadow Men and they could be anywhere. We wasted enough time, let's go."

I still had questions but knowing what was out there and coming for us - for me - I didn't want to waste anymore time. I removed my hand from his arm. We left the washroom and headed to the main room where Benjamin picked up his saddle bag from where it laid across the back of a chair. Judy was there, her hands folded in front of her chest and worry written all over her face.

"Are you sure you have to go now?" Even as she asked the question she knew the answer.

"We have already over stayed our welcome," Benjamin responded. I noticed that Judy had a small drawstring bag in her hands. Looking outside the window the sun was still high. Benjamin was wanting to cover as much ground as he could. I didn't see the old man anywhere. "As it is I don't know what will happen to you because we were here."

He sounded concerned at that fact. I wondered if Judy was more than someone he knew, or had been kind to him before. She approached him and placed the bag she carried in his hands. "Take this. I had intended to fix you two a meal but, I guess you have to take something to go instead."

There was freshly made bread in that bag, I could smell it and that only made my mouth water and stomach growl. Judy held Benjamin by the elbow and gave him a sad smile before she looked at me a moment. "You take care of her," she said.

"I will. Thank you." He said.

She nodded at his answer and came to me, pulling a heel of bread out of a pocket on her apron. "Take it, child, and keep yourself well." She gave me the bread and internally I was overjoyed. "Stay with Benjamin. He'll keep you safe." The way she said it, I had to wonder if she knew about me and where I was going, or something else.

"Yes, Ma'am. You're too kind." I said in reply.

Benjamin tapped his foot. "Scotia."

"I'm coming." Taking a large bite of the bread I followed Benjamin out of the house. A moment later we were back upon the horse and riding out of town, heading northeast to Certima.

CHAPTER 10: TYLAN
= Risky Business =

When I woke up my ribs were bandaged, again, and a grizzled man was sitting next to me spreading a foul smelling green paste over my wrappings. I tried to get up and the man pushed me back down on the wooden table that served as my bed. Surrounded by half opened jars of herbs, surgical tools and wrappings, this man was likely a healer. "Don't get up yet. I'm not done and you're not ready," he scolded and removed his hand to continue what he had been doing. His voice was raspy, like a person who has spent too much time with a pipe, and his stringy white hair was missing in patches, but his hands were strong and steady.

The pain in my chest and jaw were a reminder of the mistake I had made of accusing First-Master Sanjean in public that night we were attacked by the Lotarians in the forest. I didn't regret what I said, only the way in which it was delivered. I still thought that he knew more about the Lotarians than he was saying.

Despite my pain I got my elbows under me and pushed up to get a better view of my surroundings. The only light came from small slivers of daylight that squeezed in through boarded up windows in the back and candles that were placed here and there about the room. Odestan was the only other in the room with me aside from the grizzled man.

"If you don't stay still this will never set right." The man complained and slapped my bandaged ribs. I growled at him. I was already hurt, I didn't need some hoary headed man taking jabs at me. The man wasn't big - he didn't even look thick - I could probably snap him without thinking about it even in my broken state.

"Would you stop with the hitting!" I snapped at him.

"If this is how you treat your physician I should leave you to rot." The man said with a grunt.

"He's right you know. It's not like the physician back at the School," Odestan added in his two cents while talking around his half eaten apple. "You're not going to be able to get up easily from this." He nodded to my wrapped up chest.

With an aggravated sigh I laid down flat on the table once more. I knew they both were right. I could barely get myself into a sitting position. "Doesn't matter." I said that as much to them as I did to myself. Taking a deep breath I gritted my teeth and started to get up again.

"Hells shadows!" The man cursed, harshly setting down the bowl he had in his hands and pushed me back down on the table. He used a force that I wasn't expecting from a man of his build, and my back hit the table hard. The old man had strength in his arms.

"Watch it!" said Odestan as he got up from his chair, but the man wasn't listening to him. Trying to fight against him in my current state was not an option anymore. There was no mistaking the pain that was written all over my face and the defiance in my eyes.

"You get up one more time and I'll tie you to the table!" Yelled the grizzled man.

Odestan pulled back on the man's shoulder. "Come on, back off. He's calm."

"I'm calm," I lied. I wasn't calm but I wanted him off my chest.

The man was quiet for a moment, looking between myself and my friend, then he let up and went back to his paste. "You have to stay still for a while so that the mixture can do its job." The grizzled man explained in calmer tones. "If you don't, the infection will only spread and there won't be any help for you." Then he mumbled something under his breath that I didn't quite hear. Infection?

"What type of infection?" I didn't remember being cut, First-Master Sanjean had only knocked me down. I didn't get cut when we were in the woods, I would have remembered that.

"There was a small cut on your right side, about a couple inches." Odestan said with a small shrug of his shoulders before he took another bite of his apple. "Like a scrape from a branch or something. You wouldn't have noticed something small like that."

He was right. Small nicks and scraps didn't exist for students of a Masters School, these things happened all the time. Unless we were bleeding or unable to move it wasn't given much thought.

"The only reason we found it is because Cathem had to bandage up your ribs. You cracked a few during that tousle with First-Master Sanjean."

"You mean he cracked a few." I mumbled.

"Either way...." Odestan continued on, "when Cathem took off your tunic and started to clean you off he noticed it. Whatever it was that scratched you the tip of it was position. After a few hours you started running a fever and going into convulsions..." He trailed off and waved the hand with the apple around.

"Fortunately for you the physician was able to make something that seems to be working to combat whatever it is that's in your system."

I backtracked in my mind the events of what happened in the woods to see if I could recall when I could have possibly been scratched. I remembered that I tripped and my torch landed in the bushes. That's how I saw the Lotarians. Perhaps it had happened then and I was to in shock at what I saw to notice.

Antone had fallen during our retreat back to the village. Hopefully he was dead and not transformed into a Shadow Man. If he was, then we may have to fight him eventually.

"Did anyone else get hurt?" I couldn't have been the only one, out of the whole group, to have gotten struck.

"Only you." Odestan said, displacing my theory.

"How could I have been the only one?" I questioned. "Where are the others? Get Kaleo." I didn't try to get up again but turned my head and looked around the room. "Maybe everyone should be checked." We didn't need anyone in the group to be compromised.

"Tylan. Tylan." Odestan took up his seat and tossed the finished apple core across the room to a basket. "They're not here."

That didn't make any sense. "What do you mean they're not here? I need to speak with Kaleo before we leave."

Cathem looked hard at what he was doing with his fingers in the bowl. He was trying so hard at keeping his gaze anywhere but on me. Odestan didn't move from his chair. I wasn't anyone that he had to listen to but I assumed he knew the importance of this. And I wanted to talk to Kaleo and tell him my reasoning for accusing the First-Master.

"I told you already, they're gone Tylan. First-Master Sanjean and his Cabal. Kaleo and the rest of the Tyro. They all left four days ago." Odestan stated. The expression on his face was calm, though I could tell he wasn't lying.

"Fo-four days!" I sputtered, not believing what I had heard. "Four days! It was only a few hours ago when we got back!" My breathing got faster and my head was buzzing. They left? "How could they have left us behind? We didn't fall behind, I was injured!" It was my own fault. I should have kept my mouth shut back there instead of accusing First-Master Sanjean of sending us out there to die.

Deserters. That's what we would be labeled now if we didn't catch back up to our group. They knew I was hurt, perhaps there was a chance for me. And Odestan. *He could have gone. Why dud he stay?* There was a small stipulation in the Code that said if a man was injured in battle to where they were a danger to the rest of the group, he was to be left behind in a safe or secure location. With the trouble this village had with the Masters and the Lotarians, First-Master Sanjean considered this a good place to leave me?

"You were in pretty bad shape, Tylan." Odestan said.

"Lucky to still be alive, you are." was the addition added by Cathem.

I closed my eyes and simply focused on breathing, one deep breath at a time. I needed to clear my head. "Why are you still here Odestan?" I asked curiously. "Was there something wrong with you?" He wouldn't have stayed behind voluntarily. There was nothing about leaving a man behind to tend to the ill. If Odestan stayed voluntarily then he'd be labeled a deserter for sure.

My friend wasn't quick to answer. In the low light of the room I saw him look down to his folded hands that rested between his knees and tap his foot upon the ground. A few moments of silence passed as I laid there on the table watching him, waiting for an answer. Finally Odestan stood from his seat and motioned to the door. "Cathem, could you give us a minute?"

The grizzled man looked at me and stood. "Make sure he stays down. That mixture needs to set for at least another hour before he can move. Or try to move." The last was added with a small gruff laugh and then he was out the door, taking a few of his items with him. Odestan closed the door and sighed.

My friend made his way about the room blowing out the candles and checking the back windows. He was making sure that the room was secure from any one that my try to peak in to listen or pick up words by reading mouths. Whatever he had to say he didn't want anyone else to hear. Once he was done he pulled up his chair next to the table and sat right on the side of my ear. His back to the door. "Do you remember how you met me?"

It was a question I didn't expect, and I didn't see how it related to anything. "In the training arena, like everyone else." My brows were furrowed, trying to figure out what he was getting at.

"It was during a mass fight. One of the boys had been picking on another and it escalated until all of us were fighting someone just for the fun of it. Pretty common. This larger Fledgling had you on the ground, but right before he could punch you in the face again, I took him out from behind." Odestan spoke and I remembered what happened that day. It was foggy, but it was there. I remembered looking up and seeing Odestan offering to help me stand.

"We became friends then," I said. As much as people were friends in a place where everyone and anyone could attack you at anytime. "I was about eight."

After that day Odestan was always somewhere near me. We were in the same group of boys so I never thought anything of it. Some of the boys formed their own groups, mostly for survival sake. They were called friendship alliances. I had been in the school the longest and didn't have enough trust in anyone there to last in any friendship alliance with a group. The only one I had was with Odestan. We trained together, and often suffered the same consequences. In fights against others he always helped me out when the odds were too high and I would returned the favor.

"Everyone is in the school for some reason or another." Odestan continued. "They want to make a difference. Their parents send them, they have nothing better to do with their lives. They want to change their fate. Whatever." Odestan shrugged. He was very casual for something that required secrecy. "The males of my father's line have been training at the Schools for generations to prepare for what is coming. When I met you at the school that day I knew right away who you were, Tylan. You're a second generation Shaitae, and a male. There are no male Shaitae, or Ma'Tradoms as we call them now. Do you know why?"

Truthfully, I had never thought about it. *Shaitae*, I thought, *that's what the Lotarian had called me in the woods*. I shook my head.

"I don't know either. There are theories, but they are ones that I don't I want to get into," he said.

Then Odestan pulled down the top of his tunic and exposed his left shoulder. I saw the marking that I had always assumed was a tattoo - it wasn't uncommon for the people of the Southern Kingdom - where he was from - to tattoo themselves or even their children when they were born. His marking was that of a lightening bolt being held in a tight fist. It could almost be mistaken for a Masters Mark.

"I am Odestan of House le'Cree. A Marked One, I have the ability to heal at a rapid pace." He fixed his sleeve and covered up the marking. "It's my duty to make sure you survive until the war."

He was saying things that I hadn't heard before. What were the Houses and who were these Marked Ones? Seeing the confusion on my face Odestan scooted closer and lowered his voice as he began to explain.

When the Shaitae first came to the Realms, over 500 years ago, they were a great aid to the people. They were able to do wondrous things that we could only imagine, tapping into what's known as the Kenisis. After awhile they tired to control the people and take over, the Lotarian threat only put their agenda on hold. Once the new enemy was defeated the people were afraid that the Shaitae would try again to take over the Realms.

After the Shadow War, a group of merchants and smiths traveled to the Lands Beyond the Sea. They went looking to find aide to keep the Kingdom safe against the Shaitae. After many months they returned with items that were said to able to control a Shaitae's ability. And they were right. Armed with confidence those men took their items and meet with the Shaitae leaders. These men called their group The Houses. It was during that meeting that the Shaitae formed the Order of Ma'Tradoms and a treaty between the Houses and the Shaitae was formed.

Each of the founding men of the Houses was given a special mark placed on them by the High Ma'Tradom as a symbol of their agreement. This mark increased the bearers natural ability, made them stronger, faster, more dexterous. The one thing no one expected was to discover those gifts were hereditary. In every generation that followed a male born into one of the Houses was born with the mark that the High Ma'Tradom had placed upon their ancestor. However, these males possessed a special abilities, some of them not quiet unlike Shaitae ability. These children were called the Marked Ones.

The Houses, not knowing what the Ma'Tradoms would do if they knew a male possessed similar power to theirs, kept the identities of the children and what they could do in the strictest secret. They believed that one day the Lotarians would return and that it would be up to the Marked Ones to help save the Realm.

I scratched my head. "So what you're saying is that I'm suppose to destroy the Lotarians?" I couldn't believe what I was hearing.

"Along with your sister and mother, yes." He said it so casually. He could have been talking about the weather.

I didn't even know who I was anymore. I was this new and strange person that I knew nothing about.

Odestan shook his head. "The Lotarians came here to take over the Realms, the same thing that the Shaitae were going to do. Expand their territory and feed off the innocents just as they did before. The Lotarians are soulless creatures that can only survive if they are sustained by the spirit of others." He explained. "They won't pick and choose. Normal people have spirits too, not as strong, but the Lotarians don't care. We're on the eve of another war, Tylan. It's time we took our stand."

Even through all of that, Odestan kept his nonchalant tone. He gripped my shoulder. "I have to get you to Certima and Governor Rycliff. He's one of the last remaining Houses and the strongest. He should know more on what to do about the Lotarians. Your mother and sister will also to be there, if they make it."

If they make it. I was amazed at the thought of seeing both of them again - more happy over seeing my sister than mother who never came to visit me. I couldn't remember my sister, not even what she looked like. I only heard from my mother through a couple of letters and in none of them had she ever mentioned anything about the Lotarians or our involvement. Although, if there were Shadow Men lurking about then it was probably for the best.

"What will happen once we ---" My words were cut short by the sound of something falling outside the room door followed by hurried footsteps. Both Odestan and I looked at the door.

"I'm going to take a look." Odestan said. He got up from his chair and went to the door, opening it slowly and casting a glance outside.

No one was outside the door but on the floor I caught a glimpse of a broken plate with a wedge of cheese and a cup. Odestan wore a frown when he turned back around to face me and he scrubbed a hand through his short brown hair. "I need you to really focus on healing yourself. And quickly. We need to leave as soon as we can. Even before that. Someone was listening."

"A Shadow Man?" I asked. Who else could it have been as the Lotarians were not able to come out while the sun was still up.

"Shadow Men. Slavers. Mercenaries. Anyone who's looking to make a profit. I'll tell you one thing, I don't think the children being taken was an accident. I think that old man sold them to the Lotarians for their souls. When the Shadow Men came for the children the people put up a fight and Tomas played along." There was ire in his voice when he said that. Odestan came from a town in the South that was a major market for the slave trade just as the Eastern Kingdom was known for trading throughout the Four Kingdoms and the Lands Beyond the Sea.

"How long has it been? Cathem said I wasn't suppose to get up for a while, you even backed him up on it."

"That was before I knew we had a spy. There's not a lot of daylight left and we're both going to be in trouble if you don't get off the table and start moving."

Even if I managed to sit up I wasn't in shape to run any time soon. Odestan was at my side helping me to slowly ease to sitting position. It was hard going and I clenched my jaw hard to hold back the pain. "Who else besides you, knows about me?"

"Can't be sure. Probably the High-Lord Master knew, otherwise I don't think he would have taken you in the school at such an early age." Odestan was right about that. At least that part made sense. "Maybe First-Master Sanjean."

"I knew it!" I said before I cringed. I sat up the rest of the way with help from my friend and got my legs to hang off the table. I held my ribs with my arm and breathing was coming slow and strained. "That's why he sent us out there to die. He must have thought he was protecting the rest of the group." I was sure of it now, though the question would be why. "What about you? Does he know about you too?" If they knew who Odestan really was, then he was in as much danger as I.

"I don't think he knows. Or anyone. Except whoever was listening at the door." He helped me to my feet and it was a slow walk over to the door.

If there was someone in the village who knew, we'd be worth a lot more to anyone who may be looking for a prize. "We'll have to get a horse for you." I didn't argue. In my current state I could barely walk let alone fight.

We opened the door and stepped out into the main part of the house and found it empty. Good. In short order we were out of the house and looking around the back for horses. Thievery was against the Code and it bit at me deeply as we started to saddle the horses we found in the stable. There was no time to find the man and ask if we could borrow - or buy - the horses, and on top of that, he could be the enemy. No, we had to do what we could and get out. Even so, I had an awful feeling in the pit of my stomach.

Odestan helped me up on my horse. I felt that I could ride as long as I maintained a good hold on to the reigns. "Something is not right here." I said warily.

"I feel it too, which is why we have to hurry. Normally I'd tell you to loosen up, but this time I agree with you." That he worried did nothing to settle my own fears.

Odestan saddled up and we were ready to head out of the stable when a large shadow came across the open stable doors followed by it's owner. It was a Master, and not one from First-Master's Cabal. He was joined by two more men of the same size. They had to be Shadow Men. The feel about them was cold and dark.

The middle of the three spoke in a deep, rolling, voice. "Someone needs to be reminded of the Code."

CHAPTER 11 : TYLAN
= Shaitae =

There wasn't anywhere for Odestan and I to run, and in my current state I was more a hinderance to my friend than an asset. The three Masters blocked our exit. We couldn't leave without going through them. I cursed my luck. I cursed myself for being so stupid as to accuse First-Master Sanjean as I had those days before. If I had not done that, Odestan and I wouldn't be in the situation we were in now - facing off with three Masters and myself hardly able to get on a horse under my own power.

Just seeing the Masters made me angry. No, not Masters, Shadow Men. They had tossed aside everything that the Masters and the Code stood for to join with the Lotarians.

"Don't over react, Tylan," Odestan's warning to me was pointed and low, though we both knew that the three of them could hear it - they were too close not to.

My friend was right, but I had to wonder if being turned into Shadow Men made them stronger than I knew they already were. When you achieved the rank of Master you were marked again by a Ma'Tradom - just as was done when you advanced to Tyro. Undoubtably these men were stronger, faster, and more powerful than us. If Sanjean had wanted to I knew that he could have killed me that day with a directed blow to the chest.

Unfortunately for us, I doubted these guys were going to hold their punches. Odestan got off his horse and stood in front of mine, pulling his double-bladed axe from its sheath and holding it easily in his hands. "The three of you are a disgrace to the Master seals," he hissed out those words, fingers flexing on the axe's handle. "That you still wear them spits upon us all!" He had told me not to overreact, but it was him who was getting angry. I wanted to help him.

The Masters laughed and began to close the distance between them and us. Their weapons were drawn. Two of them had swords and the bigger, heavier set man, had a spiked mace. Unless a miracle happened, Odestan wouldn't be able to fend off all three. "Put down the toy, boy," laughed the biggest man. "We're suppose to bring you two back alive, though that doesn't mean you have to be fully functioning."

Alive? Someone wanted us alive. I couldn't think of who that would be, and how would I know when I was just learning about the Lotarians. Maybe we were to be a latest set of Shadow Men.

"Never." Odestan spat back before he gave his axe a threatening twirl and charged the closest Master.

He moved fast, faster than I had ever seen him move before. The sound of weapons clashing rang out in the stable. It was three against one and while my friend was doing fairly well at the start, I knew it couldn't last. I felt completely useless sitting there upon the horse.

On the back wall I saw a bow with a few arrows laying in a very worn casing. I didn't know if they were any good - the bow could be out of commission and that's why it was there - but it was worth a shot. While the three were focused on Odestan I slid off the horse and slowly made my way over to the bow. One of the Masters saw me. Suddenly I had a fight on my hands.

I didn't have my sword, but was quick to grab my dirk, that was still sheathed at my side, and just in time. The Master tackled me and we both cried out in pain as we hit the floor. Me because the fall on the hard dirt floor had damaged my already broken bones, and him because my dirk had sheathed itself in his stomach. He was stuck over top of me. My blade dug deeper and his blood poured down over my hands and body. But that did not mean the fight was over.

The Master pulled himself up from my bade, but I lifted my arms to keep pushing the dirk in. He began pounding at my face and my nose broke. My own blood began to pool in my mouth. I pushed with all the strength I had.

The Master was yanked off of me. My only weapon still lodged in the man's stomach. I was completely spent and on the verge of blacking out. Roughly I was pulled to my feet and forced to stand as one of the remaining Masters held me up. The larger one stood in front of me, his face dirty, but other wise he looked okay.

"Hells eternal, I should cut out your heart out and stuff it down your throat!" He punched me in the stomach after he spoke and blood spewed out of my mouth as well as any breath that I had left. My body felt like a rag doll drowning in pain. We had lost, clearly. I barely made out the body of Odestan laying face down on the floor.

"Lets get these sods on the wagon." He spat at my face and wiped his mouth with the back of his hand before picking Odestan up by the leg and dragging him out of the stable.

Our weapons were gone and the body of the man I had stabbed was left behind to bleed out on the floor. Odestan and I were tossed in the back of a small barred wagon. My friend looked like a bloody mess - I doubted I looked any better. He told me that he could heal, but he look pretty bad to me. I couldn't see much but as the wagon moved away from the village I saw Tomas standing near the outskirts. He was leaning on his staff and held his head up, a smile on his face and a pouch hanging off his belt. *Traitor.* We had tried helped his village and he betrayed us. I would not forget.

##

My body hurt so badly it was a struggle to breathe. I concentrated my efforts on not passing out, but had periods where I blacked out. I wanted to stay awake and see where we were going and possibly an opportunity for us to escape. They didn't tie us up and for that I was thankful. Odestan was breathing easier than I was right now but he was still asleep. They must have hurt him really badly. I hissed in agony when the wagon jumped from a bump in the road. "Odestan." my voice sounded weak and broken. "Odestan. Wake up."

"Hells eternal," he said with a grumble, cursing while pushing up on his elbows. Odestan spat blood out on the floor. He sat up then wiped the blood off his mouth with the back of his hand. I couldn't see too well, my eye was still swollen shut and the only light we had was what was being given off by the moon and stars, but Odestan looked more bloody than hurt. "I failed that time. Won't let that happen again." He coughed once more and I thought that his voice sounded better, even if he was keeping his tone low.

There wasn't much separating us from the driver besides a make-shift wooden planked wall. Made sense, as if that were barred, like the rest of the wagon, a prisoner could reach out and choke the driver as a means of escape.

Odestan crawled over to me and checked my wrappings for damage. I grunted and clenched my jaw hard against the pain. Hopefully the driver wouldn't think any more of it than me making sounds due to the ruggedness of the road. "This is bad," my friend said with a shake of his head. "You're not dying, but you may as well be. You're ribs are broken again and I believe one is puncturing one of your lungs."

"Since when were you a physician?" I asked, a bit of humor in my voice to give an ebb to the pain. Turns out there was a lot that I didn't know about this man.

He didn't pay attention to my quip, instead he was feeling about his person. "They took my dirk."

"They didn't leave us with anything." I missed my sword. I had claimed it for my own when we left the School and now it was probably in the hands of those Shadow Men Masters. I doubted that I would ever get it back.

"We will have to do this the hard way then. I'm going to try and heal you."

I blinked. "You said you could heal yourself," I said, strained breathing lacing my words.

"Well I never tried to heal anyone else, attempting it would obviously give me away. I don't know if it will work, but it's worth a shot. I'm already in much better shape than you. I'll be fully restored within the half hour," Odestan explained. "We can't get out of here unless you're able to move without killing yourself in the process. We might as well try."

They were suppose to bring us in alive and I felt a hairs breath from death, hanging on probably from sheer willpower alone. That Master had not been kidding when he said we didn't have to be functioning.

It was a done deal to Odestan and he kept his hands pushed against my chest. "It's worth a shot." He said again, though it sounded like he was convincing himself that trying something he had never done before was a good idea.

I scrunched up my face and closed my eyes, partially because I didn't think this would work. Neither of us said anything. Aside from a bit of warmth coming from his hands I didn't feel anything.

"Well?" He asked me a few moments later.

"Well what?" I said, opening my eyes now.

"Do you feel any different?" Odestan prodded me for an answer and removed his hands.

"I feel sick." That was no lie, I felt terrible. My stomach was churning now and my head was swimming. I rolled over to the other side and threw up the contents of my stomach - which was hardly anything at all.

"It didn't work." My friend was disappointed and I heard him sigh and knock his head back against the wagon bars.

I drew in a deep breath and coughed a few extra times, trying to get the foul taste out of my stomach out of mouth.

"Wait a minute. I can see." Amazed at such a small thing. My vision wasn't perfect, but I knew that I was seeing with both eyes once again. "I can see. My eye. It's not swollen shut anymore."

"It's working!" Odestan was so loud with that statement that the driver knocked on the wooden panels for us to settle down. We both froze, wondering if he was going to stop the wagon or if there was another up there that was going to pull back a board and see what was going on. There was a chance that he didn't clearly here the words that we said and only that we had said something.

"It's working." Odestan whispered that time, and there was amazement on his face. I was just as awed as he was at this occurrence.

"It's burning. Like, like fire," that was the only word I could think of to describe what I was feeling. My whole body felt as though someone had struck a match in my veins and the spark lit a fire that was rapidly moving throughout my system. I would compare it to the feeling I had when the Ma'Tradom touched me when I gained my rank of Tyro, only that didn't feel like fire.

When the fire got to my chest my body lurched and I heard a crack and a pop and I started to twitch. My ribs were stitching themselves back together. Since I was on the mend my friend left my side and started to examine the bars, looking for a way out. If we were going to escape we had a better chance of doing so before the wagon came to a stop.

The night was getting darker and a chill filled the air. It wasn't from the wind or the movement of the wagon. It was a Lotarian chill. "It's getting colder," I said. "They're taking us to them."

"Don't think about it," Odestan said. "You just focus on healing, it will work faster that way." Those were his instructions, and since he would know better than I, that is what I did.

"They had to get us in here somehow, but I can't find a door," he said. "Maybe there is one on the top."

He wanted me to concentrate on healing, but I could not continue laying against the bars like a rag doll. There was still pain when I moved, only not as much a before. I got to my knees and began feeling around on the floor boards for a release. There was nothing. "I have a thought," I said. "What if the only opening is in the front?" It was a possibility. The front section was the only part without visible bars.

"If that's the case then we have a problem." Odestan said. Sighing he went to the boards and eased against it. There was give. Not only in that one, but the one under and above it as well.

Odestan whispered. "It's tricky, but there's not other option." He was thinking.

"We can't push the boards to the side, he'll notice," I said.

Odestan shook his head. "Not to the side. Forward. If he's sitting in front of the boards, and we push them, we could knock him out of his seat. Even off the wagon. It will work. He's not expecting it."

We were both speaking in low whispered tones, and hoping that the sound of the wagon and the horses hooves on the ground helped to hide our words. "He thinks we're both to beat up to do anything, we have the full advantage here. You should be well enough to help."

Easy for him to say. I could still feel my body burning on the inside as I continued to heal bit by bit. I took in a deep breath and stretched my arms, not sure how much my body could take while it was repairing itself but it I didn't want to wait around until we reached our destination either. Besides the night was getting colder. The longer we waited the more we risked being surrounded by Lotarians. My friend knew it as well, I could tell by the look that I saw in his eyes. It was decided. We would do what it took to get out of the cage.

I prepared myself for what was to come and placed both of my hands on the wooden boards. "Okay. Let's do it."

Just because the boards had a bit of give when Odestan tried them earlier did not mean they would be easy to move. Anything could be behind the wood, even a chest. If luck was on our side this would work out as planned. We would push the boards, hit the driver, and gain freedom from the cage. If not, then we would have a problem.

"On the count of three....." Odestan began the countdown. "One... two... three!"

Both of us pushed hard on the middle of the boards. It broke away from the others and hit the driver who yelled out in surprise. But he didn't fall out of his seat.

"What in blazes!" The driver smashed his back against the other boards and it pushed us back. "They're trying to escape!" He yelled. He had to be yelling to someone. Now that he knew we were trying to escape there was no turning back. It was now or never.

Odestan and I rammed against the rest of the boards, pushing harder as the driver started to bring the wagon to a stop.

"Quick! We can do it! Here we go!" Odestan shouted. The both of us revved up for another push. "NOW!"

We pushed at the boards as hard as we could. We were making progress. It was two against one and the driver couldn't push against us with the same amount of force as we were giving out. The boards were not sealed together and the top board fell.

"Keep pushing!" I yelled, and that's what we did. We had nearly enough space to squeeze through when one of the Masters we had faced in the stable came running up to the cage on horseback. It was the one with the mace and he smashed his weapon against the side of the wagon, causing our cage to rock to the side and us to fall to the floor.

"Get back!" he yelled, taking another hit at the cage with his mace.

With the rocking of the cage Odestan got another idea. He threw himself at the side of the cage, causing the wagon to rock more on its wheels. I understood what he was doing and followed his example. We were going to turn the wagon over. It was risky, but if it worked it would throw off the driver and our way of escape would be open. Then we would only had to get through the opening before the Masters got to us.

Trying to keep the cage steady, the Master with the mace reached out and grabbed it. His sudden pull, and miscalculation of his weight, caused the cage to fall in his direction. What luck! The wagon fell over, even the horse neighed as he went to the ground.

We had crushed the Master under the wagon. His horse was getting up and starting away from the scene. The driver had been thrown as well and was currently tangled in the nearby bush. This was our opening.

Scrambling on the rails we kicking at the Masters hands and ran for the exit and the horse. Without it we wouldn't be able to flee fast enough before we were caught again. Reaching the horse first I grabbed its reigns and pulled myself up with a bout of strained effort, Odestan helped me the rest of the way and got on behind me. We pushed the horse hard down the path.

It wasn't long before one of the Masters was chasing us down upon the another horse. I could hear the fast beat of hooves on the ground. My heart was pounding in my ears and going so fast I thought it was going to pop out of my chest. It had been cool in the wagon but now it was down right frigid.

"They're getting closer!" Odestan said, he was holding on tight and looking behind us, as well as around.

"The Masters?" I asked. I had only heard one horse and didn't think that the Masters would double up.

"No. The Lotarians."

That's what I thought he was going to say, but I had hoped against it. I tried looking into the darkness of the night, but I saw nothing. Without a light I had to trust the horse to not run himself into a tree. *What I wouldn't give right now for some light.*

We simply went, pushing the horse to go faster and faster. The horse bucked suddenly and Odestan and I were almost thrown from it's back.

"It must have seen something!" I shouted.

"There's nothing there!" He said back. But the horse had been spooked and would not go. I flicked the reigns, trying to urge it forward, but it didn't work. The more I prodded the more he bucked and cantered backwards.

"It's no use. They are here and he knows it." Odestan said. "We need to run."

Lotarians were there and we couldn't see them. There was only the darkness and the cold. Odestan got off the horse.

"You go. They only want me." I said, thinking that I would stay behind and give my friend a chance to run. I still wasn't fully recovered - I was probably at the best I would get with the little work Odestan had done. The escape had taken a lot out of me and I could already feel the pain returning.

"Don't be such a fool!" Odestan said and he grabbed my arm. He was going to pull me off the horse if he had to. "They'd want to kill me just as much as they want to kill you! Now let's go!"

Stay on the horse and try to get it to move, or get off and run. Neither of them were ideas that we had time to think about and both had possibilities of failure. The horse, if it would run and stop acting like a fool, would be a great tool. We could really use the speed but that wasn't something we could rely on right now. I got off the horse and Odestan and I ran.

Up ahead of us our path stopped in front of a black wall. We skidded to a stop, both of us panting hard and placing our backs to each other. "That's not an ordinary wall." Odestan said, though it was something we both knew. It was the Lotarians. Looking around that wasn't the only wall. We went to the side and saw the same thing.

My body was so cold that I was shivering against my friend. "We're trapped," I said. I may have felt defeated but my voice still had strength. "We are surrounded."

"Shaitae! Shaitae!" This time that name wasn't being called by simply one Lotarian, but it echoed around the black wall that was steadily closing in on us.

"There has to be a way out. It's not going to end like this!" Odestan took up a fighting stance, poised to fight them off with his bare hands.

I went on the offensive as well, knees bent, legs shoulder width apart, hands up and eyes focused. Only it was hard to focus on one thing when everything was darkness. There were enough of them that one couldn't be distinguished from the other and all around 'Shaitae' was heard.

"It's not going to end like this," I said through grated teeth. "It's not going to end like this!" With each word I said my determination to get out of this situation was growing. I was just beginning to learn who I really was. Tomas, the old man of the village, needed to pay for what he did. Not only to us, but to the people of his village. First-Master Sanjean risked the lives of everyone in my Tyro trying to get rid of me. There were Shadow Men in the Schools that had to be outed. Odestan risked his life to save mine. My sister, my mother, they were waiting for me. *People are counting on me!* I was not going to die here, helpless in the woods!

My hands were clenched into tight fist, knuckles white and nails nearly piercing the flesh of my palms. "This is not the end!" I shouted at the top of my lungs to the Lotarians and anyone else who may have been near. My voice echoed in the stillness of the night.

Energy flared up inside of me. The weariness I had, the lingering pain that was in my body, all of it was now gone. The only thing I felt was the burning surge of energy that manifested itself in a blue and white flame that encompassed my hands. I didn't know what was happening. I had wanted light and now it was literally in my hands. I felt powerful and quite unlike myself. I stepped away from Odestan.

"Tylan?" Odestan said to me. On his face there was both fear and curiosity. The black wall of Lotarians had stopped converging on us. They had even stopped calling out the word Shaitae.

From the dark wall of Lotarian shadow, one separated itself from the mass and began walking towards me, stretching out what looked like a hand and beckoned me forward. My hands were still aglow and when I didn't walk toward the Lotarian that black wall of darkness started in on us again.

Were they not afraid of me? The thought fueled my anger even more. Just as the Lotarian I saw in the woods tried to approach me without any fear, these ones were doing the same. *I'll show them the meaning of fear*, I thought.

For a moment the white light surrounding my hands dulled to grey and my eyes clouded over and I could hardly see. Darkness. I could feel darkness wrapping around me.

Odestan called out my name and knocked me to the ground. The light from my hands circled around us and shot through the forest. Dark howls pierced the night and the Lotarians burned in the white glow.

It lasted only a few moments, but for me time had stopped.

"In all the Heavens...." Odestan swore as he got us both off the ground. The light in my hands was gone and my body felt completely drained. What had I just done?

For the second time that night Odestan was pulling on my arm. "We got to keep going." There would be time to think about what happened later. Right now we had to press onward.

CHAPTER 12: SCOTIA
= Certima =

The clothes Judy had given me helped keep me warm as Benjamin and I traveled further north along the road. During our travel he acquired a new item of his own, a small brimmed hat which he kept pulled down nearly over his eyes. I liked it. Dark gray to nearly black, it matched the black and silver trimmed tunic that he wore. Benjamin's face looked so serious and focused I'd have thought him a statue if I didn't know better. I narrowed my eyes thinking that doing so would let me see something that I had missed. *How is this guy is able to do what he did?* The answer to that still alluded me

The more time that I took time to actually think about this man - as oppose to complaining about comfort and his round about answers - I began to see that he wasn't all that bad. He may have come off as domineering and tactless, but I suppose he had his reasons - I only didn't know what they were. Besides, Benjamin was the only person I had right now.

I must have been looking at him a bit long - or hard - for he startled me when he started talking. "It's not exactly polite to stare at people. Especially if you have nothing to say."

Internally scolding myself for the flush that I knew was coming rapidly to my face, I looked away from him and paid attention to the road. Why did he always have to sound so crass when he spoke to me? "I have plenty to say," said as I pulled at my composure. "You only never want to answer."

He shrugged, I felt the movement against my back. "You have to ask the right questions to get the right answers."

Typical response from him. I thought that I had been asking the right questions, what more was there to say? Fine, I would play his game. "How do you know my mother?"

Benjamin shook his head. "Wrong question."

That was a perfectly valid question! I grumbled. This area was quiet and peaceful. We hadn't seen another person for a few miles since we passed a small farm house hours ago. The air, though, smelled like rain and I hoped that we would find shelter to wait it out instead of traveling in it. I sighed and slouched in the saddle. It didn't matter if he was easy to look at or not, he still grated on my nerves. I sat there focusing on not being angry at him or at myself for this situation.

"If you put that same effort into your Kenisis, as you do in being angry with yourself you would not have your difficulties."

I turned quickly in the saddle and stared at him. "What do you mean? How do you know about that?" I never told him about my troubles in the Kenisis, and surely mother didn't know - unless the Order had been giving her updates on my progress. Even so, why would she have told him?

"So full of the wrong questions..." He said in a nonchalant manner.

I scrunched my eyes and balled up my fist before taking a deep breath. He said that I kept asking wrong questions, I only needed to think about what I wanted to ask before I spoke. Maybe he thought I knew the answer to the things I asked already. "I've always had trouble focusing. With the Kenisis we are suppose to trust it, focus on something we can't see and believe that it will be as we want it." I spoke softly.

Benjamin said. "There is a difference between belief and faith. You know all the steps, and believe that it should work. But, as you've hardly seen results from your belief, you have no faith. Using the Kenisis is about having faith in your belief that you will get what you need when you need it. Where is your faith, Scotia?"

At first I though I had the answer to his question, I even opened my mouth to speak only to close it again without saying anything. Faith. Belief. The Ma'Tradoms always told me to believe in myself, and I tried. Aside from what I had done to stop the wagon I was a failure. After studying, and trying, for eight years at the Order and coming up short, it was hard to believe that I could achieve anything. "No one believes in me" I said meekly.

"That's an excuse." Benjamin said. Those eyes of his were looking right through me and I leaned my head back, trying in vain to avoid it.

"It's the truth," was the rebuttal I gave. "You haven't seen the way people look at me. They expect me to fail. Like I always do. "

"Blaming others for your own failings holds you back as much as your lack of faith. You're not a child. Situations will come your way and you have to choose whether or not you let it control you, or you control it." Benjamin said.

"What about now? I can't do anything about what's happening now. Or what happened to Maerilea."

"Yes, you can." His words took on an edge. "Decide to take control of your own destiny or you will never be nothing but a pawn in someones game."

Then he looked away from me, his eyes returned to the road ahead of us. I continued to look at him, at his face. What he said was echoing in my mind. Didn't he see that I was the victim here? All these things were happening to me, and to my friend, because of me. If I hadn't eavesdropped at the chamber door we wouldn't have been locked in that room back at the Order, or out here scattered about in the Four Kingdoms. There were Lotarian's after me and I couldn't do anything to stop them. How did Benjamin expect me to control my destiny when I couldn't even get him to answer my questions.

##

Certima - otherwise known as the 'City of Light' by many - was the largest city in the Eastern Kingdom. It was also the richest in all of the Four Kingdoms and was rumored to have main control of the Realms even when it was not the Kingdoms turn to house the King's Chair. Though I had read of this place and what it held I was still in awe at what I saw as we neared. Sometimes what you read and hear can bear no comparison to reality.

On the outskirts of the city were vineyards, that was one of the main staples of this Kingdoms economy. The grapes that came from Certima, and the wine, sold at the highest value. Much of the higher sales came from to the Lands Beyond the Sea. The smell of wine filled my head and made me dizzy even before I could see where they were.

We were joined on the main road by other people who were traveling to the inner city. A large wall constructed out of white marble stones and mortar surrounded the inner city. Along the wall were anchors for torches. In the bright sunlight the white marble seemed to shine. Walking the wall battlements were the Kingdoms Soldiers; it is said that they were the best trained and disciplined men outside of a Masters School. Every Kingdom had them. Only a small handful of the City Guard and Battle Men were chosen to join the Kingdom Soldiers. These men wore silver plated armor, and the visors on their helmets was pushed upwards so the face could be seen.

Over their armor was a white tunic with the crest of the city embroidered on a large circle in the middle. Purple sky with a blazing sun and a trade boat in the center, the crest was an interesting design. Could Benjamin be a Kingdom Solider? It was a valid thought. I was looking at him again, trying to affix this new bit of information somewhere in my reasoning. He could be. I didn't think that it was impossible.

"You're already drawing attention to yourself," Benjamin spoke in a low, soft tone. "If you keep looking like that you're only going to attract more."

I didn't know what he meant until I took a good look around me at the people we passed. Many of them were watching me. Some of them even whispered to the person they were with. Others bowed their heads or tipped their hats to Benjamin when they saw us pass. It was the eyes that were a bit unnerving to me. Feeling self conscious I tried to disappear into my clothing and Benjamin's arms that were on either side of me.

"Why are they looking at us like that?" A valid question in my mind and one that I hoped he would answer. Of course, he didn't. Benjamin kept the horse going at a steady pace towards the Governors Palace and I did my best to ignore the looks.

##

It was odd to say that a place sparkled, but that is what the Governor's Palace did - it sparkled. The gate that surrounded it had small mirrors on spikes and a ring of lamps surrounded it. Those mirrors reflected the light of the lamps, making a ring of bright light around the grounds. When those lamps were lit there wouldn't be anywhere for a shadow to hide. The walls were white marble with gold accents, polished to give off a sparkle and shine as well. It was all simply amazing.

Members of the King's Guard were posted at the top of the palace gate and at its opening. As Benjamin brought the horse to a stop near the gate two of the guards approached us. One of them had a very pronounced chin and he kept his eyes on me. There was something about his gaze that was unsettling. It wasn't hard and cold, like Benjamin's eyes, this man's eyes felt cruel and it made me feel cold. The other man had age lines along his eyes and mouth and his skin was leathery. Both mens hands rested by their sword hilts.

"State your name and purpose," said the older guard.

Benjamin picked up his head and tipped the brim of his hat upwards to take the shadow off of his face. It was amazing that any part of him could have a shadow considering the amount of light the lamps and mirror pieces were giving off at the gate, but it did.

"Lieutenant Servat" he said in his calm tone.

The Lieutenant turned his head to the side to look at Benjamin and then scoffed out a laugh. "Lord Daniels, it is you!" Lieutenant Servat exclaimed.

Lord Daniels? I tried hard to hide the look of shock and surprise that was clearly on my face.

"They said it was you. I didn't recognize you with out your, you know, arrangement. How pleased we are to see that you have returned." said the lieutenant. "Should I call ahead for you? Though I have a feeling that your arrival is already known to the Governor as well."

This man, Lord Benjamin Daniels, had more things to him that were yet to be seen. Was he one of the City Lords? Why would he be sent to look for me if he was? It didn't make sense. Men like him had people to send out to do work as simple as retrieving someone. It made sense now why the people of the city looked at him so when we came in. Did the people in that other town know who he was as well? More over, did they know that he could do the things that he did?

I looked between the two men before I simply lowered my head, all the better to hide the shocked expression that still registered on my face.

"I'm sure he knows," Benjamin said. "Have there been any Lotarian sightings around the city?"

"Yes, Sir. Since you left there seem to be more of them that come to the line outside the city walls. They never try to enter, they only wait." The lieutenant explained.

"And the citizens? They are abiding by the curfew?" Benjamin asked.

"Yes, Sir," Lieutenant Servat said with a nod of his head. "No one is outside city gates when the sun goes down. Those in the farm lands have been properly equipped for their safety."

Benjamin pulled on the reigns to the horse as it had started to stamp it's foot in impatience. "Very good. Gather the men. I need to meet with the other Lords before it gets much later."

All of it was very interesting to me, listening to them talk and trying to figure out what all of this was about. Clearly the Lotarians were gatherings around the city and I understood now why Benjamin kept the pace he had. From what the lieutenant said, it seemed that the Lotarians were amassing in number. Especially around the city.

The man with the chin had been silent the entire time, but never once did he take his eyes off of me. I wished that he would. I couldn't take his cold look for much longer. The feeling he gave me was also gravely uncomfortable as though there was something wrong. We were safe inside the city, it must only be my imagination and flashbacks from the slaver. My memories of how he looked at me back in the wagon. I shuddered at my own thoughts and before I knew it the horse was kicked back into action and we were going through the gates. I looked back at the guard as we passed by only to see that he was still staring at me.

I tugged on Benjamin's sleeve to get his attention. "That man. I got an uncomfortable feeling from him." I confessed in a hushed whisper. Benjamin only nodded to what I said, but I felt that he took me seriously.

We pulled into the stable that wasn't too far in from the inside of the gate. Even in here the area was lit, though not as much as the outside had been, it was still well lit. I started to study the people I saw, especially the Guards that patrolled along the walls. I didn't feel anything to strange from them, but I still had an odd feeling in the pit of my stomach. That was when I remembered Benjamin telling me that the Lotarians had Shadow Men - people they had captured and now worked for them. It could be possible that there were such men amongst the King's Guard, or even the servants. This was a scary thought.

"Don't stare too hard, you'll only make them suspicious." Benjamin whispered to me. Perhaps he had the same thought as I - that not everyone here was what they were making themselves out to be. If that was his thought, he didn't show it.

After we dismounted and Benjamin handed the reigns over to the stablehand, he took hold of my arm the way a gentleman would when escorting a lady and we walked up the steps that led to the main doors. They opened for us and we went in. The palace was large and spacious on the inside. Double stairways were on either side and made of white marble and ivory. The main color theme was purple and gold, just like the crest that was on the guards' tunic. I felt slightly under dressed as I saw that even the servants had a higher quality of clothing on than I, even if it was in the same design.

We didn't take the steps, instead we continued walking straight on through. The servants that we passed bowed or curtsied to

Benjamin and gave quiet words of greeting as they went about their task. The Order was large with many rooms, but the feeling about it was calm. This place made me feel small and vastly insignificant. It could have only been my imagination but I sighed all the same. *The sooner we get to our destination the better.*

As we rounded a corner there was a beautifully dressed woman in following silks and dangling jewels. She was walking down the hall in our direction, accompanied with her entourage of ladies who were not as finely dressed as her but they all looked very lovely. Her skin was the color of milk and her black hair was in a bun tied by golden cords. A golden collar, with the city crest in the middle, was around her neck. This woman had to be one of Governor Rycliff's wives - he was said to have three. I didn't think she could possibly be a slave because of the other women around her.

Benjamin's arm tensed the closer we got to the lady and his hold grew tighter when she left her entourage to come up to us and boldly take up his other arm and walked with us. She hardly spared a glance at me. The women who accompanied her now walked behind us. To say that I was shocked would be an understatement. Not only shocked at her boldness but that Benjamin did not do anything about it.

"Lord Daniels, you've picked up a stray." She said teasingly. Her voice had a high pitch to it. She turned her gaze to me and I wished that she hadn't. This lady was appraising me with her eyes. "And what a scruffy little thing she is too."

"Scruffy!" I yelled. I may not have been as richly dressed as she was, but I was hardly scruffy!

"Clarissa." Benjamin interjected, though his voice held amusement. "Isn't there some poor Stewart that is pinning for your attention?"

I would not sulk in front of this woman. I huffed and paid attention to where we were walking, taking notice of the art work and designs in the hall.

Clarissa waved off Benjamin's comment and gave a small laugh. "But I've been without you for weeks." She was talking to him but I could feel her eyes looking directly at me. She was probably gloating over the reaction I gave. "That little thing has had you all to herself," Clarissa whined.

What did she think Benjamin and I were doing the whole time he was gone? Benjamin sighed and stopped walking when he came to a set of large wooden double doors. "You can't be without what you have never had. Now, I believe your husband is expecting me."

There were no guards outside of the double doors, something I thought to be odd. Maybe they were inside. There had been some posted in various places inside the palace but not here.

Clarissa groaned and let go of Benjamin's arm. She stood next to the door, her arms folded in annoyance. "That he sent you all around the Four Kingdoms to find her is insulting to me and the other wives." She sucked her teeth. "Well, I guess she doesn't have to be pretty."

"I could say the same about you," I said, tossing my shoulders back and lifting up my head, trying to be confident like the Ma'Tradoms I saw in the Order. "Why else would you need to hide behind all those jewels."

Clarissa stared at me with eyes full of venom. She opened her mouth to say something but Benjamin let go of my arm and stepped in from of her and reached behind him for the doorknob and turned it. The door opened with a click and he then pushed it in to allow me to go through. Benjamin had made an effective barrier between myself and Clarissa. She had taken her eyes off me to watch him instead.

"Seems that the little girl has bite," he said to her before he ushered me into the room, leaving the Governors wife outside the room.

Little girl. Is that how he saw me? It pained me to think that he thought of me that way and I had to reminded myself that I disliked this man and should not care what he thought. I was going to see my mother and brother, and finally find out what was going on.

The room we entered was a large office with a desk at the back, and chairs on either side of it. Bookcases and vases lined the walls, and the curtains were closed over the windows. Light came from the hanging lamps in the ceiling and wall mounts, there was even had a lit fire place stationed along one one wall with plush seating safely around it. I had expect to be going to the large receiving room that I had read about. This room felt fit for intimate, private settings, as I supposed this was.

"Mother!" I saw her right away, standing on the right side of the desk. She looked well. In a dress of dark red and gold, she looked more like Ma'Tradom than she had when I last saw her. Even her Ma'Tradom cloak was about her shoulders. I wanted to run over to her but I stayed by Benjamin, maybe if she was the only one in the room it would have been otherwise. There were so many things that I wanted to ask!

Governor Rycliff sat behind his desk with two of the King's Guards at his side. He rose as and he looked tall and imposing. The black beard on his face was peppered with white but there was strength in his jaw as well as in his eyes. Slightly round in his belly, he was as richly dressed, perhaps even more so, than Clarissa. He motioned us forward and the guards at the back closed the doors.

"Thank the Heavens you have finally arrived, Scotia," said the Governor. "Welcome to Certima."

CHAPTER 13 : SCOTIA
= The Key =

"Governor," Benjamin spoke up. He was watching the two guards who were at the desk. They had yet to move from their stations at either side of it. He nodded his head toward them. "Have those men, and the two by the door, wait outside. Then we will speak." He put his hand on my shoulder and squeezed. He didn't want to me to step from him.

Governor Rycliff chuckled and looked at his guards. "You may speak freely in front of them, Benjamin," he said.

"Then you don't need her." It was the no-nonsense attitude of Benjamin's that I was use to and he turned away, directing me back to the doors.

"Alright, alright." the Governor said. Benjamin and I turned back around. "Wait outside until this is over," he said to his guards. "You're probably making the girl nervous."

Without a word the guardsmen started to file out of the room. Benjamin turned to keep a barrier between myself and them. My Mother approached me and Benjamin released me into her care. I smiled at her, thankful that she was alive. She took one of my hands in hers and with the other she touched my face, lifting up my chin and examining me.

"Are you alright?" she asked in a soft whisper. I only nodded for the moment as she had my jaw in her hand. Everyone in the room was being cautious. There was a strained tension in the air that only dissipated once the guards exited and the door closed behind them. After that my mother embraced me - much to my surprise - and held me tight. "Thank the Heavens you're okay."

It was the most expression I had ever seen from her - from any of the Ma'Tradoms. I was quite surprised. It took me a moment but my arms closed around her too and I felt her warmth.

"There are Shadow Men in the Schools, and in the city" Benjamin said once the room was secured. I looked at the faces of Governor Rycliff and my mother to gauge their reaction to what was said. I couldn't read anything off of either of them. "I found Scotia in the back of a slavers wagon being guarded by some of them."

"All the better that you found her when you did." Rycliff said. He stepped out from around the desk and held out his arms in a welcoming gesture. The Governor continued, "But how can there be Shadow Men here? In my King's Guard? Ridiculous. Every man would give their life for me."

"If Masters can be converted, what makes you think that your King's Guard are any different?" said Benjamin.

Pulling away from my mother I looked around the room. Someone was missing. "Where's my brother?" I asked. Turning to my mother for the answer. "Benjamin said both of you were going to be here?"

There was sadness in my mothers eyes and she looked at Benjamin who gave a small shake of his head. My mother brushed a hand down the back of my head. "He hasn't made it here yet." It was the safe answer to tell me. "He's coming."

"He better hurry," remarked the Governor. "I sent a message to the High-Lord Master requesting that he send Tylan here two weeks ago. He should have been here by now. Getting to Barq is a lot quicker than traveling all the way to Ravensbro."

"If he's not here by now, then he may never make it." Benjamin said.

The shock and surprise was in my voice. "You said that he was coming. You told me that he was going to be here!"

My mothers eyes questioned Benjamin, but he didn't answer - no surprise to me - and then she looked at the Governor. "We can do it without him." She said flatly.

"No!" I ran to the Governors desk and leaned forward on it to look the man straight in the face. I was going to pleaded with him if it got results. "I don't know most of what is going on here, but he's my brother. We need him. Don't we?" Whatever this was that they needed me for I had been told that he was needed too. Now they were changing their plans and still not telling me anything about what was going on.

"The situation has been compromised." Rycliff explained. "There are Shadow Men amongst the Schools, you heard what Benjamin said. Your brother could be one of them. Or even dead."

"He's not dead! He's not a Shadow Man either!" I said coming to the defense of a brother I could barely remembered. "We have to go find him. If he's at one of the Schools, and Shadow Men are there, then he's in even more danger."

"It's too risky, Scotia. We have you, we can do without him. Try to understand, we can't loose the both of you. If we did then the whole of the Four Kingdoms will fall into the hands of the Lotarians." Governor Rycliff said.

"There is no way of knowing if he's been changed not." My mother agreed. "Governor Rycliff is right. We can't take the risk."

I couldn't believe what I was hearing. "It's so easy for you to toss us away isn't it!" I yelled at her, turning my anger on my mother. *She doesn't care None of them do.* "You act like you're so happy to see me, but what about him? Are you just going to leave him out there like he's nothing!" It was so easy for her to abandon us. I had already lost Maerilea, I couldn't willfully give up on my brother.

"Benjamin?" I appealed to him. He was my last hope. "Benjamin. Come on. Please. You brought me here safely, you can bring him here as well." Benjamin would not look at me. His eyes were trained on the Governor. The room was very quiet.

I stood close to Benjamin and nervously grabbed his hand and tipped my head back so I could try and catch his eyes. "Please Benjamin?" I whispered. "Please. The Lotarians will kill him."

The Governor shook his head. "We don't have time for this. The ceremony will take place, as planned, in one week. Benjamin, take her to her room." Came the order.

"No!" I shouted, "We have to go look for him! Benjamin!"

"Scotia, go with Benjamin. You don't know what you're saying." said my mother.

If they were not going to help me, then I was going to go myself. I let go of Benjamin's hand and made for the door. I was quickly caught and in the presence of the Governor and my mother, Benjamin once again picked me up and tossed me over his shoulder like a sack of wheat and made his way out of the room. I kicked and hit at him, but just as before, they were ignored. "You can't treat me like this!" This was embarrassing. I couldn't believe what was happening.

"Take care of her, Lord Daniels," Governor Rycliff called after us as he and my mother followed to the office doors. The guards were there waiting, but they didn't move to help or speak to the situation. "She's in your charge."

He only nodded and carried me while I continued to protest. In my struggles I noticed one of the helmeted guards was looking at me and a chill went down my spine.

##

Ma'Tradom Airtia stood next to the governor and watched as Benjamin took her daughter away from the office kicking and screaming. There had been something unsettling about the meeting that had taken place, besides the possibility about what may have happened to her son. She closed her eyes and sighed.

"What was that? I didn't quiet here what you said," Rycliff said. He had leaned in towards the Ma'Tradom and had placed a finger against the back of his ear.

Under normal circumstances he wasn't the type of person Airtia would associate herself. He was to greedy for his own good, and it wasn't solely in money. Each one of his wives was younger than the next. She didn't want him getting any ideas when it came to her daughter. When she found out that he was one of the remaining Houses that still knew the history, and even had something that could help in the upcoming war, she almost considered taking her chances alone. If it were not for her children that is what she would have done. It would have been to chancy. With the high number of Lotarians in the Realms and the Shaitae bloodline getting thinner in the Ma'Tradom ranks they didn't stand a very good chance. As things stood they would be weak without Tylan, but that was something she would deal with at that time. If she had to smile a bit more to get what she needed from Governor Rycliff then it was a small price.

"I simply mused about the wandering eyes of your men."

The governor chortled heartily. "There are some things that the road cannot hide. Wouldn't you agree?"

Airtia watched the governor as he went to sit back behind the desk. "We only have one key, and if her brother has been taken we have no room for error. You do know how to use it, don't you?" It was a game of tag with the questions the two of them spewed back and forth. She didn't trust that he really knew what he was doing, and he didn't trust her in general. A healthy relationship when it came to politics.

Rycliff huffed and rustled through his desk, pulling out drawers and misplacing papers as he looked for something. "There is a reason why this is the last strong House," he said, taking a moment to fix the Ma'Tradom with a stare before he continued his search.

Out of the eight Houses that had started off, Rycliff was the last of three. The other Houses died out, though most of them were destroyed in Kingdom Wars for the King's Chair. He was a direct descendant of the original founders and had acquired many of the objects that the original founders brought with them that were able to be used against the Shaitae. He was also a Marked One. Though, like his ancestors before him, Rycliff kept this secret from any of Shaitae blood. "I know who to trust and, unlike your kind, I don't go parading what I have around and lording over everyone else. Here it is." He pulled out a small narrow wooden box. There wasn't anything special about it, in fact it looked quiet plain.

Airtia approached the desk and waited with anticipation for him to open the box. During the Shadow War the Shaitae had used the Kenisis to create these keys. They increased the Shaitae ability. The creation of the keys were the main factor in ending the war. But the amount of power that the Shaitae surged through the keys was said to have not only destroyed the keys, but the Shaitae who were connected to it as well. Governor Rycliff had said that he had such a key in his possession. The Ma'Tradom had never seen one of the keys and wanted to see if he was telling the truth. Rumor had it that they were all destroyed.

Silence fell between the two of them. Airtia waited patiently but Rycliff did not make any further actions to the box. "Well?" Airtia said rather impatiently. "Open the box. Let's see this key."

Rycliff wore the slightest of smiles and leaned back in his chair, entwining his fingers and laying them across his large middle. "I don't think so."

"What?"

"If I understand my history right - and I'm sure that I do - the Shaitae made these keys to increase their power. Using it destroyed the Lotarians and laid waste to everything in the area." Rycliff said, a smug look coming over his face. He tented his fingers and let out an exaggerated yawn. "Who's to say that I show you the key and you don't go crazy, destroying my estate?"

"What's to keep me from doing that anyway?" Said Airtia.

There was a hint of truth to what the Governor was saying. There was a limit to the amount of Kenisis a person could draw before they were affected mentally and physically. The more complex the Kenisis the more it wore on the wielder. The keys let the person connected to it draw as much power as they wanted for as long as they wanted. Even until it destroyed them like it had those Shaitae.

The governor reached for the box and placed it on top of his stomach and folded his hands over it for security. "Then I suppose we'll have to trust each other."

##

Benjamin carried me through the hallway. He didn't stop or even miss a step as I kicked and pushed against him to let me go. He was using that same hold he had used after he rescued me from the slaver wagon. He had to be made of stone for all the response he gave to my protest.

The people that we passed on the way to the stairs, and up them, didn't say a thing about what was going on. Many averted their eyes or quickly shuffled away even after I appealed to them for help. They didn't seem in shock at the sight, and that made me think that something like this wasn't out of place in Certima - or at least in the Governors Palace. At the top of the stairs we took a right and went down the corridor where I saw another one of the governors wives walking with her entourage. Upon seeing them I stopped protesting out of embarrassment. Who knew what Clarissa may have already told them about me. There wasn't a need to give them more reason to turn up their noses.

Benjamin opened the door to a rather large bedroom. All I ever had at the Order was a small room big enough for a plank bed and a desk with a chair. Compared to that, this room was massive and for the moment the scope of it put me in silence. Large windows covered one wall, and they were covered with elaborate drapes that sported the governors colors. There was a large post bed with enough pillows for me to drown in, a chaise, lounger, small table with a couple chairs, even a door that lead to my own bath. The room was warmed by the fire in the hearth and the air smelled like lilies, a perfect match for the warm autumn tones of the room.

"This is amazing...." I said in surprise. I had momentarily forgotten about the conversation that had gone on in Rycliff's office, that is until Benjamin tossed me off of his shoulder and into the sea of pillows on the bed.

"Wait! Wait!" I called out while picking myself out of the pile. "Benjamin. You are going to go find my brother, aren't you?" He had already started heading to the door but stopped when I started talking. "Please?" I would say it a hundred times if it would get him to do what I asked. Close to begging, but I would.

His answer came at first with the shake of his head. "There are things at work here that you don't understand."

"Don't tell me that I don't understand!" I yelled, throwing the first pillow I could get my hands on at him. "You got me here. You did your job. I can't do mine unless I know he's okay." It was true, I didn't know my brother well, but he was family and I felt alone. If he were here with me at least there would be someone and maybe he would understand. "You told me that he would be here. How am I suppose to feel?"

"Grateful." He said, sitting himself down on the chaise, one leg propped up and the other lazily draping the ground. "If your brother has been converted into a Shadow Man then he would kill you as readily as the others."

"You say that like you don't care what has happened to him." I stayed where I was on the bed but I studied Benjamin. Sitting there he looked tired. Perhaps he was and maybe he would fall asleep. Then I would be able to sneak out of here and go find my brother on my own.

"I care about what happens to you. If both of you were here it would be better, but we can do with the one. And your mother."

I frowned deeply. "You speak of me as if I were an object. Is that all that I am?"

"You should clean yourself. Take advantage of this time while you can."

He didn't answer me. He never answered me. I could read between the lines and what he really said is that I was an object. I had begun to think that he might actually have liked me to some degree considering all he did to protect me. Even in the office where we were supposedly safe there was something in his demeanor that spoke of a readiness to spring to action and save me from the governor, even my own mother, if the need arose. Maybe I was imagining things.

I pulled in my lower lip and looked down at myself. I wasn't that dirty, I had taken a bath at Judy's house before we left, but that had been a few days ago. Sliding off of the bed I took my time going to the bathroom, casting a glance at him here and there to see if he was watching. He wasn't. His head was against the back of the chaise and his eyes were closed, the hat on his head pulled down to cast a darker shadow over his eyes.

"Are you going to stay here?" Putting the question out there as I recalled he told the lieutenant that he wanted to talk to the other Lords.

PAST'S PROLOGUE

Benjamin had both legs on the furniture now and crossed his arms across his waist. Shrugging his shoulders he answered, "Don't worry, I'm not going to barge in on you this time."

"At least that is comforting." It was a quip. He was referencing to the time he had come in last time I was bathing.

When I got to the room I saw everything that I needed, and was surprised to see that a bath had already been drawn. Servants must have done it while we were in the office for I didn't see anyone leave the room. I gathered the towels and soap, turning them over in my hands, and peeked out to check on Benjamin. He looked to be sleeping. *Wonderful*, I thought, *I'll waste a few minutes and then sneak out.*

The bath waters were inviting though, and the scented steam coming from the top called to me. It may even be easier for me to walk through the palace clean rather than looking scruffy, as I had been called. With a sigh I decided to bathe.

Disrobing I stepped into the water and almost immediately felt the stress I had been carrying start to melt away. I could allow myself to rest, for just a little bit. There was a lot of information to take in and I couldn't even pretend to understand it fully. I needed to be well rested and prepared if I were to sneak past Benjamin and out the palace.

I sunk down deeper in the tub until the bath water covered my head. I thought back to all my studies at the Order and my lessons about the Four Kingdoms and the war with the Lotarians.

CHAPTER 14: TYLAN
= Turning Point =

There was no telling how far we ran, all I know is that we kept going. I hadn't heard anyone coming after us, but neither Odestan or myself wanted to stop for assurances. Even when it seemed that our legs would give out from exhaustion, or our lungs would explode from the strain of heavy breathing and lack of air, we kept going. We stayed off of the main road and away from any people or houses that we happened to see.

It was few hours yet until dawn when we finally came to a stop. Odestan spotted a small lean-to that was partially dug into the ground. It had a small narrow opening and did not look like much, but it was sturdy and could be well defended. Odestan and I crawled inside and collapsed on the ground, doing the best we could to return a steady flow of air to our lungs without breathing to heavily.

Our dwelling was small, it was likely made for only one person, not two. The rugged thatch did not allow for much light. If the Lotarians and Shadow Men were looking for us perhaps they would overlook the lean-to due to the size, but if not we would try our best to defend it. What we needed was a fire but to do so would pinpoint our presence like a beacon, but at the same time it would give us a weapon against the Lotarians. Night wouldn't last forever, so I kept my thought to myself and choose to think about what had happened back in forest instead.

"We may be safe here until dawn," said Odestan. "But shouldn't chance it. We can stay here an hour, two, three at the most and no more. Then we should keep going towards Certima. We need to get rest while we can. There's no telling what will happen now."

He was right. and I nodded my agreement. "Can you do that?" I asked him suddenly.

"Can I do what? Get some rest? You'd be about it too if you know what's good for you." Was his response.

"You know what I mean. With the light. The thing that shot from my hands. What was that?" I asked, hoping that he would have some answers but Odestan was shaking his head. "I've never heard anything about a male being able to harness power until you told me about guys like yourself. Marked Ones."

"What you did back there isn't anything that I've heard of before," Odestan replied. "The other Marked Ones, we may have abilities, yes, but nothing that's able to kill a Lotarian. Not like what you did." Odestan was settling on the ground and trying to get comfortable in our small space. "Look, you may as well forget about drilling me for answers because what I told you is all that I know."

"I'm going to check on our position," I said before crawling out of the lean-to. I already had a vague sense of the direction we were traveling, but I had an unsettling feeling and wanted to have a look around.

I couldn't tell too much but I could see the stars and learning to get your position by them was one of the lessons taught at the School. By their position Certima was to our left. That was where we needed to go. I didn't see, or hear, signs of us being followed, but just because I didn't see them did not mean they were not there. The only thing I trusted was the absent of the Lotarian chill in the air. I went back inside and found Odestan was already asleep.

I had so many questions and there wasn't anyone to provide the answers. Amongst the concerns about my newly discovered heritage were the ones about the Masters Schools. There involvement in this didn't make any sense, it went against all the things that we were taught about dealing with the rest of the world. The Schools stand outside of the system. We are the protectors of all. That is what we were told. Governors couldn't hire us to fight in their wars, and we couldn't become part of the King's Guard. What could have made those other Masters back at the town turn against the Code? I even wondered which school they were from. Too many questions and not enough answers.

I needed to clear my head of those thoughts so that I could sleep. I was as tired as Odestan and we needed time to recharge before heading back out. Just a few hours, that should be enough and then the sun would be out and we could make faster progress without being wary of every shadow in our path. I propped a few sticks of dry wood and debris against the opening of our small shelter before settling down next to my friend. Before I knew it, I fell asleep.

##

It seemed like only minutes had passed before Odestan was nudging me awake. I opened my eyes. It was still dark out but I could see the sharpened point of a spear hovering inches away from my nose. That was not the only thing I saw. Our shelter was gone, only the wall I had been laying on remained. Odestan stayed very still for he too had a spear in his face. We were surrounded by a group of fully wrapped, dark cloak figures. For a moment I thought that they were Lotarians, but there was no chill and I could see their eyes. It was the only visible feature. Each of the figures that surrounded us had a weapons trained to strike.

"Who are you?" I asked. "What's going on?" Perhaps they were Shadow Men and were going to hold us captive until the Lotarians arrived. No one answered to my questions.

"What do you want with us?" I tried again but the result was the same. I saw Odestan start to move. He immediately stopped after the spear that was trained on him pressed down between his eyes.

"Tylan Sacony?" questioned the one in front of me holding the spear. The sound of the voice was slightly muffled through the covering over the mouth, but it sounded feminine.

I was shocked. Not only did this stranger know my name, but they knew my last name as well. It had been so long since I had heard it that I had nearly forgotten it myself. Who were they? "Yes? That's me," I cautiously admitted.

Whispers ran through the group that surrounded us. The spear tip that pressed against my nose slid down across my face, nicking my cheek and stopping once it reached the middle of my neck. Trying to escape the spear I leaned my head further back into the wall but the spear tip only followed. I dared not even swallow now for fear of cutting my own throat.

"Know my name, Tylan Sacony," said the one with the spear. "I am Ori'Zyia of House Raeth. With your death, I shall bring an end to this war."

====The end of Book One====

PAST'S PROLOGUE

27136639R00080

Made in the USA
Charleston, SC
03 March 2014